WHEN YOU GET DOWN TO IT, we don't even know what's on Dominique's mind. She might have been mad at 7:52 then forgot all about it by 8:52 and by 11:52 be smacking her hand declaring a beat-down on the lunch lady.

A whole lot can happen in one hour. How many hours are we in school? Eight? Nine? That's a lot of hours to be hot about nonsense. And isn't that the point? I don't know what any of it's about. I don't know if Dominique is playing or not, and why is that? It's none of my business.

JUMPED

RITA WILLIAMS-GARCIA

Quill Tree Books
An Imprint of HarperCollinsPublishers

Quill Tree Books is an imprint of HarperCollins Publishers.

Library of Congress Cataloging-in-Publication Data
Williams-Garcia, Rita.
Jumped / Rita Williams-Garcia. — 1st ed.
    p. cm.
    Summary: The lives of Leticia, Dominique, and Trina are irrevocably
intertwined through the course of one day in an urban high school after
Leticia overhears Dominique's plans to beat up Trina and must decide whether or
not to get involved.
    ISBN 978-0-06-307928-1
    [1. Conduct of life—Fiction. 2. Bullies—Fiction. 3. High schools—Fiction.
4. Schools—Fiction.] I. Title.
    PZ7.W6713Jum 2009   2008022381
[Fic]—dc22   CIP
                                                                                    AC

Typography by Alison Klapthor and Catherine San Juan
21 22 23 24 25   PC/LSCH   10 9 8 7 6 5 4 3 2 1
❖
First Quill Tree Books edition, 2021

For the memory of my father,
James Jasper "Russell" Williams,
who gave me my first pair of boxing gloves

CONTENTS

I

Zero Period

LETICIA

ZERO PERIOD. You got that right. Fail one math test and you're up before the first "chirp" of day. Up before streetlights turn off and sun rays shoot through the blinds. Fail one math test and you're stepping over a snow-covered homeless lump to get to the stop, shiver, and wait for the city bus to pull up to your boots.

None of this had to happen to me. None of it. Having to set and wrap my hair at 8:00 pm instead of 10:00. Making "Celina" wake me because my alleged alarm clock won't do what it's supposed to do when it's supposed to do it. Getting dressed in the dark because a hundred watts are too hard on my eyes at 5:45.

If not for those missing 13 points, my mornings would be calm, not chaotic. A 52 on the final and they wouldn't pass me. They couldn't scrape up a point here, half a point there to make up the thirteen. They said SHOW ALL WORK in the test booklet, so I did that. I showed them my sides, my angles, line BEC bisecting line DEF. I did my part. What was the sense of showing all that work if they had no intention of doing their part? The missing thirteen are there in the booklet. Had they dug deep enough, they would have found them. I would have passed.

Mr. Jiang knows he doesn't want to see my face this spring semester. I aggravated him fall semester like he aggravated me. This was all on him. He should have done the right thing for both our sakes and passed me along to Geometry II with Miss DeBarge.

Why Bridgette or Bernie didn't handle things immediately, I can't understand. Neither took time off from their jobs to confront Mr. Jiang or strike a deal with the guidance counselor. No. They just let Jiang fail me. Bridgette shook her head and Bernie dipped his biscuit into the gravy but no one gave Leticia a second thought when all they had to do was show up. Speak up. Do what they were supposed to do.

Anabel Winkler's grandmother loved her. Anabel's grandmother talked to the guidance counselor and fixed things so Anabel could attend summer school after this semester. That's why Anabel is still wrapped up tight in her Hello Kitty comforter crunching Z cookies.

If someone loved me, I'd be turning over in the warmth and safety of my queen-size bed. But no one thought to open the envelope addressed to the parents of Leticia Moore that offered the choice between summer school and rising at an ungodly, unsafe hour in the chill of near night. I know the school sent the letter. The school's very good about mailing letters to the house, and Bridgette and Bernie are usually pretty good about reading them and following up with the "talking to." Bridgette and Bernie knew to look out for the letter from the guidance counselor's office. They knew it was coming. They signed the blue booklet with the big 52 on the cover under *Parental Signature Mandatory*. But when the guidance counselor sent it, and the postman delivered it, the parents of Leticia Corinthia Moore, aka Bridgette and Bernie, didn't bother to open the envelope. They just fed it to the recycling bin like it was a bill. That's right. My do-not-pass-go card was recycled into toilet paper and Starbucks napkins, not doing anybody a bit of good.

It's not enough that I have to get up before the world turns and watch newspaper chunks hit the streets and block-long McTrucks unload McFood crates. I'm stuck watching gears of the working world shift just so I can take an "extra help" math class I get no credit for. It's like being in school for free. Like working behind a counter without getting that nine twenty-five an hour. Or nine fifty-five. Whatever next-to-nothing they pay kids to dodge french-fry grease. Except you get up, risk your life waiting in the dark to sit through slow-motion Geometry and get no credit. Two periods later you're still repeating Geometry I, still looking at Mr. Jiang's face, and he's still looking at your face. You get nothing for being in "extra help" math before the world turns. For all this chaos you get zero. Period.

I dig down in my bag for my schedule but the lady cop waves me through. She knows my jail sentence and my big face by now. Zero period doesn't miraculously disappear from your schedule. Once a class is stamped in the column that's grayed out for everyone else, you're stuck. You're a zero-period regular and the cops know it and wave you through.

Miss Palenka isn't a full teacher. She's still in college getting her practice on us, probably getting paid zero, and that's about right. But she's nice, wears okay outfits, and takes her time explaining until everyone looks like they got it. For the next twenty-five minutes I'm present, taking notes, breaking down the proofs until ten minutes before the bell rings. By then everyone is arriving, congregating outside, and I can't write another "given." To us stuck inside, the milling and laughing sound like a party, and who wants to be inside when the party is going on outside?

I try to sit through it, but how many ways and times can she demonstrate a ninety-degree angle in a right triangle? How many times can she say right triangles can only have one right angle? How many times can she point to the hypotenuse? Right, right, right triangle. I got it. I got it. Please don't say it again. But there she goes, working hard for her zero.

Pen down. I'm done listening to zero for zero. I need to be outside where the dirt is fresh and the gossip is good. I need to catch it all while it's clicking and flashing: what they're wearing, who they're with, and what they're saying. I need to sashay myself within twenty feet of Chem II James and let him get the ball rolling. Can't do that from inside here, so I scribble a bathroom pass right quick and raise my hand.

Can you sign my bathroom pass?

Miss Palenka points to the clock. I have to wait

until the bell rings. She's determined to be that firm no-nonsense high school teacher, hip to all the tricks.

I can't hold it, I say. And I'm squeezing my thighs and sliding from one end of the chair to the other. It's a standoff: she's acting tough, and I'm acting my ass off.

The minute her chest collapses and she heaves that sigh, I rush up there and shove the slip of paper under her nose. There is nothing to acting. If you have parents, you're a natural-born actress. I'm out the door like pee is shooting out of me. You know I have my bag with me and I'm not coming back.

I don't run this fast for gym, but the thrill of getting out and being in the mix has got me trotting like a fat cop on foot in a TV chase scene. I get to the nearest stairwell and stop. Not these stairs. They'll lead me too close to the front. Too close to the hall patrols. Instead I go all the way to the back, side stairwell. I'm so happy to be on my way outside, happy to get out of zero period, so happy to be at the top of the stairs. I take one, maybe two, steps and—

Oh my God

2

Stretch, Roll, and Go

TRINA

PRETTY, RIGHT? No two browns alike. Squeeze some red, some yellow, black, vanilla, *naranja* into brown and you come up with pretty people. *¡Míralo!* Nice and dry. Ready for the gallery.

Mixing comes natural. It just ought to. Not only am I mixed to perfection, I have aptitude for art and colors.

What would that school mural look like without truly, truly yours to add life? The walls would look like the walls at my old school: a couple posters of ash brown Dr. King, Rosa, Malcolm, and the gang to greet you in the morning. But hang my art on the mural, you walk down C Corridor and—*¡vaya!*—Black History Month, but colorful. Pretty. With a point of view. And that's what I do. Add color, my crazy point of view, and—*bam!*—I make you look twice.

Reds for Malcolm—get it? Harlem Red. My Harriet, stopping traffic in greens and yellows. And my Rosa surrounded by hot pinks and cool pinks—Rosa *sin* roses? Don't be ridiculous. What?

Gotta get there before everyone. Show Mr. Sebastian where to put Malcolm, Rosa, Harriet, and Dr. King. Check it: surrealism. "I Have a Dream" that looks like a dream. Mr. Sebastian will go crazy.

Don't get me misunderstood. I don't love being up this early, but for me, no problem. I don't do a lot to look this way. My lucky gold chain hangs around my neck, asleep or awake. A quick shower, a spritz of Passion Pink, my killer outfit laid out ready for me to jump into. I just stretch, roll, and go. Yeah, yeah. Rocking the hot-pink warm-up suit because all eyes will be on me. What? Don't hate because I got it like this. Kisses to Mami— *mmwack*—still snoozing. Thanks for hooking it up, Mami. I didn't have to come out all gorgeous.

In case you're wondering, that's not conceit. It's just fact. It's like when you see a Picasso—those colors, those shapes, those crazy mixes—and you hear the music in the paintings, you can't help but say, "That's dope." When people see me, they see walking art. They pause because the hair is bouncing, the light brown eyes are twinkling without trying, the skin is caramel and crème, the *galletas* are shaking, the body's untouchable tight. What? They can't help but stare or step up. No milk mami tatas, no big legs, no fatty patty on this rack of perfection. Who needs extras when you can stretch, roll, and go like this?

Whether I glide down the street, across the way, or down the hall. Nothing to weigh me down. If I want to skip like I'm six, I skip. If I want to run like Road Runner—beep-beep, *tchong*! But I'm not conceited. I'm not cold. I leave the lookers with the famous Trina shaky-shake. You can't catch me, but I give you a little treat and everyone's happy.

I'm a crowd pleaser, custom blended. Half Latina with a little this and a little that. It doesn't matter which what, like it doesn't matter if a girl has a blue eye blinking this way and a green eye blinking that way in a Picasso. It's all about the colors, the mixes, the shapes, the music. Like me. Color. Mix. Shape. Music.

Oh, I've seen it go wrong. I've seen it go totally wrong. Your mother thought she hooked it up, but you come out a Ripley's Believe It or Not! sideshow. Your mother thought you'd have long Hawaiian silky, but you got Brillo puffs. Your mother thought you'd have golden brown skin, Bit-O-Honey skin, vanilla crème skin, and surprise: your mother's greasing blotchy red, ashy dull skin. Or your forehead is too damn big, or your nose don't go with those cheeks, or your lips are too pink for the skin. It can go wrong. Like I say, horribly, horribly wrong.

People always ask, "What are you?" trying to figure out all the mixes. Instead of "I don't know" I say, "One hundred percent Trina." Go ahead. Ask. How much time, how much money I spend on hair? Answer: next to nil and hardly *nada*. Shampoo, conditioner, blow, and go. What? My hair is like my face, is like my body. Good to go, so why mess with it?

Officer DaCosta can use a shot of joy. She can't be happy, wearing that navy blue uniform every day. No color. No shape. No variety. Don't she wish she could wear this hot-pink joint or something like it? She is navy and black from head to toe. Silver-plated badge, nameplate, white stripes on her sleeves. When she stands you can see her accessories on her belt. Club, cuffs, radio, thick writing pad, space where a gun would go. Wears flat black cop shoes. Her nails are square and unpainted. No rings. No jewelry. No makeup. Not even gloss.

I arrive just in time to brighten her day. Instead of trouble, I have nothing but prettiness to show her. I peel off Harriet from my tube of painted beauties. You've never seen Harriet look so good. I gave her a green-and-yellow dress with matching head scarf instead of that gray you see her wearing in the history books. Makes sense. Camouflage, for hiking in the woods.

"I have my own spot on C Corridor," I tell Officer DaCosta, "for Black History Month. You should come. Check out the gallery."

She nods and gives me all the compliments. Creative. Interesting colors. Different. Talented. She doesn't know the artist's language, but that's all right. I translate how she means each word.

To Officer DaCosta I'm a cup of coffee, extra sugar *con crema*. Her eyes are open and smiling although she gotta be Officer DaCosta: on the job. With just a little color, a little smile, I've made her day. She nods me and my artwork through.

I have only a few minutes before the halls are flooded. I don't want anyone else to get a sneak peek. Can you imagine all those adoring kids going crazy for my artwork? They might tear the paper or smudge it trying to get a closer look. They'll crowd me and be like, "Tree-na, hey."

* * *

I almost can't stand myself. I have that sugar-rush hyper feeling because it's my day. I'm already a standout, but today I'm set to star.

I'm bouncing along, my artwork in hand, and then I ease through these girls where B meets C. "Hey," I say, though I don't really know them. The boyed-up basketball girl barely moves. The others, her girls, appreciate the hot pink and step aside.

It's okay if they don't speak. I know how it is. They can't all be Trina.

3

Killing Time

DOMINIQUE

I PUNCH VIVICA.

Vivica punches Shayne.

Shayne punches me.

I punch Viv.

Light punches. Sweet punches. They don't mean anything. Just us killing time in the cold. Waiting for the cars to fill up the lot. No. One car. Waiting for one car to pull in.

We have business. I have business. Business with Hershheiser.

Shayne and Vivica are my girls, not my backup. Backup? I don't need backup. I handle my own stuff. Vivica and Shayne are just hanging. Being my girls.

Scotty? He's not up yet. Or he's just leaving his mother's. Scotty's a punk and a baby in the cold. *Come on, 'Nique.*

13

Keep me warm. Boy tries to bury himself in all this here, but I can't think about Scotty. I have things to handle. Important things. Can't have Scotty here. Scotty wanna be lovey, hanging all over me. Slow me down. *Need love, Scotty? Hug your mutha.*

"Hope he gets here. It's freeeezing."

I ignore them. How long it takes is how long I'll wait. Just thinking about it. How he caused this whole situation. Me, out on the sidelines. Me, out. Benched.

All the above makes me mad. Mad enough to—

Viv starts jumping around. "Oh, wow. Look at 'Nique's breath. That's crazy! See how you're breathing." Viv points too close to my face. If that wasn't Viv, boy . . . I'da blocked and blocked hard. That's from instinct. From 4th Street Court. I can't fight it. That's in me. I have hard, fast reflexes. A hand goes up, I block. Block or charge. But I'm all right and that's Viv, not a baller, so I step back, smack my fist into my other hand. Viv's lucky. She don't know. She just don't know. I coulda hurt her in a flash, so I'm like, *Chill.*

Viv's pointing at my face. My mouth and nose. How my breath shoots out in short jabs, smoky ice. That's cracking her and Shayne up.

Shayne says, "Damn, girl. You all right? You're like a bull snorting steam."

I shrug, say I'm all right. But I'm heated. Waiting. Got things to do. Business to handle. Life and death. Important.

"Let's get hot chocolate from the corner. It's cold," Shayne whines. She's Scotty in girls' jeans.

I say I don't want no hot chocolate. "Y'all can go. I'm staying."

"Then stay. Don't have none," Shayne says. She hooks an arm in and around Viv's arm. "We'll be back."

I turn away. Go. Go get your hot chocolate. They're yakking too much while I'm trying to stay focused. They think I'll let him slide by for some hot chocolate? They think I'm going to blow my shot to grab him for some Swiss Miss and hot water?

Before Viv and Shayne get anywhere I hear, " 'Nique!" Viv is heads-up loud, pointing to the gate. "Green Bug!"

Before Hershheiser can finish parking, grab his briefcase, his plastic coffee mug, I'm on him.

Hah! Got him! He's scared to leave the car. A rat in a trap. He knows what he did. He knows what he took. Yeah, Hershheiser. You know. You know. Shitting square ones, aren't you?

I knock on the window. Come out, mouse.

Finally he opens the door and comes out. Brown wool skullie pulled down tight over his half-bald head.

He's chewing like a rat, fighting to get whatever down his throat. Rat with whiskers. Up and down, up and down. No. A mouse. A rat wouldn't hide. A rat would come at me. I could respect that. I can't respect a little brown mouse.

"Miss Duncan. Why are you in the teachers' parking lot?"

Shayne and Vivica cackle hard because his teeth are rattling. He's scared and it's funny. I'd laugh too but I'm mad.

"Listen, Hershheiser," I say, "I need my grade changed."

He tries to walk fast but I'm on him. Little man, where you think you going? We 'bout the same height but I know you feel my shadow. I know you feel me sticking. Go ahead. Make a move. You move, I stick. You move, I stick. You can't run from me, mouse.

"Miss Duncan, your grade i-is your grade. You'll d-do better in your new cl-cl-class. The sec-sec-second semester's j-just starting."

"I don't want that grade. All you gotta do is change the seventy to a seventy-five. Five points. That's all, Hershheiser. Just five points and I'm off the bench."

"Look, Miss Duncan . . ."

Calling me "Miss" don't make my shadow smaller.

I'm not playing with you, mouse. Change my grade.

" 'Nique," I correct him. "Look, Mr. Hershheiser, you can do this. You can change my grade."

"Miss, er, Dominique"—mustache twitching—"you can't accost me in the parking la-la-lot. This isn't the way to do things."

"I'm not costing you. You're costing me. Costing me my minutes. My season. All I need is to be up a few points and I get my time back."

Here I am, pleading my heart out like a stupid bitch in love and he's running away. We're already up the steps to the main door. See how he runs. He pushes the door open and is relieved. Little brown mouse is in the hole, makes it to safety, in with the other teachers. The cop nods him through and cocks her head up at us: Where you going?

"Girls, you know the deal," Cop Dyke says. "Seven fifty-five. Not before. It's either on your schedule or you have to have a note. Got a note?"

We don't have a note. "That's my teacher," I say. "I'm talking to him."

"Well, he left you hanging, didn't he?"

I can't say nothing back. That's how mad I am. Mad enough to reach over, grab her club, and break it in two. Mad enough to pound the desk with my fist. The little brown mouse slides into his hole and then Cop Dyke blocks me like I'm some punk and I'm supposed to slink away with my head low. Say that's all right. You don't have to hear me out, mouse. You don't have to let me through, Cop. And then she's going to be funny too? *Left you hanging, didn't he?*

But here we are. Out in the cold because the cop won't pass us through. Viv and Shayne drop the ball completely. They can't remember why we're here to begin with. That they're my girls and they're supposed to just be here. Shayne's a baby for that hot chocolate. I'm tired of hearing her whine, so me and Viv walk her over to the bagel man on the corner. She gets hers, then I tell her, "Get me one."

"Get your own."

I'm still mad but Shayne got a way with her and I say, "Don't make me spill that cup all over you. You'll really be hot."

She knows I'm playing. She holds the Styrofoam cup out to me. I take a sip, to make things nice, but give it back. Too sweet. She and Scotty like that sweet, sweet stuff. I shake it off. It's nasty sweet. She and Viv pass the cup back and forth. They try to get me to take another sip but then they stop. They know when to leave me alone.

We start back, this time to the side door at the back

of the school. That's the best way to get in or out. The building's too big. They can't put a cop on each door. If you want to, you can break in or out.

We stand there for a while. Viv and Shayne crunch up now that the hot chocolate is gone. They talk, talk, talk but I keep my eye on the door. I wait. The janitor opens the side door to take a smoke. Then *boom*. We rush him like a storm. Oh! That's funny.

He wants to curse us so bad, grown man and whatnot. Can't be bum-rushed by no girls. But what can he do? Tall, crooked grandpa. We're too much for him, laughing like a pack of she-dogs, and it makes me feel drunk and silly.

We're in. I'm fit to charge up the stairs, the third floor. Hunt down Hershheiser. If I keep pushing on him I know I can break him. We're down in the basement at the far end of the building near the gym, near the coach's office. I have a thought. A better thought. All Coach gotta do is change her mind. She can do that. Change her mind. It's her rule: 75 and higher to take the floor. It's not the law. It's not in the rule book. She can change her mind. She can bend this one time.

Come on, Coach. Let me by this time. I just want my minutes. I'll take sixteen. Eight. I'll take four. Four minutes and she'll want me in for eight. Four minutes when we're down ten points and you'll never sit me out. You'll never bench me. Just don't make me sit and watch. Don't bench me.

I tell Shayne and Vivica to wait. I don't want Coach to think I'm ganging up with my girls. Coach don't respond to that. Coach is like, "You'll break before I bend the rules." Coach isn't no Hershheiser. Coach'll be up in your chest, standing six by six, a brick wall you can't get around. But I'm not trying to charge at her. I just need her to hear me. Just hear me out.

When I go into her office the radio's on some talk station. Sports talk. She's reading the paper, drinking coffee. Only her eyes go up, then back down to the paper.

"Coach, my minutes," I start.

"Not now, Duncan."

"But, Coach, I just—"

"Duncan, I said not now."

"But, Co—"

"Duncan. Out." And she points to the door like she points to the bench. Like I'm a dog and I take commands. She has the minutes, the game, the season, and I got zip.

Shayne, Viv. Do not speak. Don't say nothing. Not one sound. Just shut the hell up.

They get it. They read my face. They follow me from the basement up back, to the first floor where B meets C. I'm so mad I can't even see them. Just their shapes. They're not even Viv and Shayne to me. I feel hot and tight. Caged by the No box.

NO   NO

NO   NO

We're inside where it's warm but my breath comes out fighting. My chest is rising and falling, rising and falling. Just no one say nothing. Don't speak. Just let me calm myself down. Just be quiet.

Some stupid little flit comes skipping down B Corridor like the Easter bunny carrying some rolled-up paper. Skipping. Hopping. In all that pink. Cuts right in between us and is like, "Hey" or some shit. Cuts a knife right through my space. Right through it. Wearing some perfume making a pink stink in my nose after she turns on C. Like she don't see I'm here and all the space around me is mines so keep your pink ass on that side of the lane. No. She cuts a knife right through my space then turns. And I slam my fist into my other hand because she's good as jumped and I say, "Her. I'm gonna kick that ass at two forty-five."

4

On Speed Dial

LETICIA

CAN YOU BELIEVE MY LUCK? I sneak outside to skim dirt, and dirt finds me before I'm down the stairs. It's all too good to waste. Every second counts. The bell will ring in five minutes. I fold the bathroom pass down to a padded wad and jam it on the inside of the door lock. I step outside the building where the reception is good and hit 3, Bea's number on Celina's speed dial.

Bea is on the "work" part of work-study. One week classes and one week the job. Unlike us, Bea doesn't have to hide her cell phone. Her boss doesn't care about that. But here in school, they confiscate your phone if they catch you using it or if it goes off during class. Principal Bates took my Celina away and I promised Celina I would never let that happen again. I would be more careful, especially in chemistry. My teacher, Mr. Cosgrove, is funny about ringtones, especially if it's an actual song. He dances his way to the groove of the ringtone all the way down to your seat, holds his hand out until you drop your phone in his palm. That's why I keep Celina on vibrate, stashed in my bag. I wish Mr. Cosgrove *would* try to take my little girl. We'd have a custody battle in class because no one takes my sugar. Right, baby?

Celina's plastic body is cold like metal. She can't stand being outside when it's freezing, but just like Bridgette tells me, "Deal. It's only temporary." I'm not worried. Once I start talking up this fresh dirt Celina will get warm in no time.

Bea clicks and I start.

"BeaBeaBea. Girrrrl . . ."

"Ooh, what?" She knows the sound of fresh dirt dropping when she hears it. "What's up with James?"

Who cares about Chem II James now? I just spill it: "Trina's getting her ass whupped."

"Tall Trina or Cute Trina?"

"Cute Trina." Clarification needed: Trina isn't cute by my standards. Trina *thinks* Trina is cute. But Bea and I are on the same page. She knows which Trina I mean.

"Right now?" I know Bea wishes this was study week and not work week. That would be something to see. An event too good to miss. Trina getting stomped on school grounds.

"No. No," I say. "That's the thing. It's happening after school. Maybe you can get here for it. Leave work early. Tell them you need a book in your locker for homework."

Bea gasps. She can't believe it either. This is better than the tray of free doughnuts her boss puts out for the workers. She is going to miss Cute Trina's beat-down.

"By who?" she asks.

"Basketball Jones."

"Who?"

"You know. Big girl. Wavy hair. Dominique."

Bea agrees I had it right the first time. Basketball Jones. When you think Dominique, you forget she has natural waves and a nice complexion. You think girl on the ball court in the biggy-baggy basketball jerseys and shorts, if you want to call those long bloomers shorts.

"That big girl?" Bea takes a moment to picture it. Big Dominique and little Trina. She makes a sound of shock and dread. A gasp swallowed by a groan. She can't stop saying "Oh my God," and I can't stop saying "Can you believe it?"

The first bell rings but we keep talking. This is too good.

"Tell me what happened! How did it go down? What did Trina do to Dominique? Tell me everything."

It won't shatter anyone's world if I walk into class late. I start spilling and stretching the story beyond the split seconds that it occurred. I tell Bea how I got the pass from Palenka, how I ran all the way to the end of the hall to slip out the side door in the back of the building. I tell her where I was standing when I saw them, and how Trina skipped by in those ghetto pink sweatpants, and how she cut between Dominique and her girls, Shayne and Vivica, and how Dominique smacked her hands together and pointed her finger all bang-bang and that she was going to get Trina at 2:45.

Now I'm really late, but Celina is hanging in there with four bars of reception like a good girl so I keep on talking.

"But what did Trina do?" Bea asks. "Why is Dominique going to beat her?"

"Haven't you been listening?" I'm a little hot. Sometimes Bea just misses the point, which is I know something juicy and I share it with her. This is a little breakfast goodie. A yummy sausage, egg, and cheese to snack on. Instead of snacking, she's asking questions.

I say, "Because she was being Trina, doing what Trina do. You know how Trina do. Being in everyone's face. Shaking that tail. 'I'm Trina. He-ey.' You've seen her."

"And *that's* why Dominique's gonna beat her?"

"Wouldn't you?"

Bea said no. Fighting over stuff like that was petty high school mess. Funny, it wasn't petty high school mess last semester when we rode up on Jay with Krystal. It was "on" then.

Bea says it's not right and asks if Trina is crewing up or what.

"Crewing up? Bea, you serious?"

"Yeah, I'm serious, 'Ticia. What is she planning to do? Stick it out till two forty-five with her crew or cut out early?"

I'm not thinking about Trina's next move. I just got this good dirt and ran outside to share it.

I say, "Trina don't know it's going down. Like I told you, her back was to them. She was skipping away, being Trina. Then she turned down C."

Another gasp-groan. "She doesn't know?"

"That's what I said."

Bea eats up thirty whole seconds of my phone minutes to say how wrong, how trifling it is and that—get this—I shouldn't let it go down like this, and then asks again if I'm sure that Trina doesn't know.

"Don't make me say it again, Bea." Bridgette will have a fit when she sees these minutes racking up on the phone bill. A fit. I need Bea to fast-forward

26

but she's stuck on poor Trina.

"So what are you going to do, Leticia?"

"What?" I can hear her. I just can't believe she's asking me what *I'm* going to do about it.

Then she says it again, all *You heard me.* "So what are you going to do, Leticia?"

"Me? Me do what?" I can't even put these words together. How did this get to be about me?

"Weren't you the only one to see it go down?"

"No," I say. "Vivica and Shayne were right in it."

She sucks spit to say I'm being trifling. "Vivica and Shayne are with Dominique, which is as good as them kicking Trina's ass with Dominique. Come on, Leticia. Would you tell on you?"

I can't believe how she's turning this helter-skelter.

"You gotta give Trina a clue," she says.

"Why do I gotta get involved?" As much as Bea and I have shaken heads over Cute Trina being Cute Trina and now it's up to me to save her?

Bea says, "Trina can't stand up to Dominique. You gotta tell her, Leticia. You're the only one who witnessed it all go down. This is your mess."

The second bell rings and I tell Bea I have to go, I'll call later. Celina is warming up but I'm freezing. I power Celina down to save her energy for later.

5
H-o-t C-h-i-c-k

TRINA

I GIVE MY ARTWORK to Mr. Sebastian and speed along, beep-beeping, to Biology, minding my business, when Assistant Principal Shelton pulls me aside.

"Trina." He shakes his head, wags his finger.

Uh-oh. Sounds serious.

"What did I do? I didn't do nothing."

"That outfit."

Big relief! Is that what this is about? I give him my famous shaky-shake. "Cute, right? I got it at Marshall's. They only sell it in my size and that's only right because you can't wear this and be packing pound cakes. I don't care what the big girls say."

Now that that's settled, I start to walk away. Miss Womack closes the door at five after and talks real fast about polypeptides so I must be in my seat ASAP. But

AP Shelton is blocking my kick-ball-change. He's not even smiling.

"That outfit is hardly appropriate for school. We've had this discussion before, Trina."

"Yes, I know. So why you breathing on me? I'm not cut down to there." I slide my finger over my lucky gold chain and along the zipper, where most girls have cleavage. His face turns red. I make his day. This is just a little game between him and me. He knows he likes messing with me in the hallway. This time it's not the tatas popping. The bottoms on my warm-up suit hang a little low and the top a little high, almost showing my appendix scar, but that's practically invisible. I say, "It's only a little belly button and a cute one. At least I don't have an alien knob sticking out. Now that would be disgusting."

Last semester AP Shelton got me for sporting a low-cut top. But in all fairness, it was technically still summer and that top needed to get some wear before it went in with the mothballs. I wasn't offending anyone. But Shelton made Mami come up to school with a big sweater. How embarrassing! The way they threw the sweater over me was like they do on *Animal Kingdom*. The hunters spot the innocent zebra peacefully munching on a patch of grass. They creep up from behind, blast the unsuspecting zebra in the butt with a tranquilizer dart, and then throw a net over her. Only thing that burnt me about that whole episode was Mami clicking her tongue and acting outraged when she blew me kisses and said I looked cute that morning.

I pull the bottoms up a little and then tug the top down. "Problem solved?" Assistant Principal Shelton rolls eyes to the skies. Where does he begin?

"It's only flirtware," I say. "It don't mean nothing."

"You come to school to learn, not to flirt."

I laugh like we're friends and he made a funny. He doesn't think I'd take that seriously, does he?

"Come on, Mr. Shelton. This is high school. What do you think flirting was made for? Last year we socked boys in the arm, this year we hit 'em low, if you get me. It's all about flirting. Flirting's what we do when we're not taking notes."

Awww, Mr. Shelton knows he wants to laugh but he holds back. I'm winning him my way. Come on, Shel-E-Shel. Crack a little gap below the mustache. You know you want to.

Nope. Still tight.

I dance for him, a stomp and shake I borrow from the Boosters. "Look. Arm, arm, leg, leg, belly, tatas covered. Happy?"

When I finish turning around for him he says,

"Trina, I can read *hot chick* on your, your . . ."

He actually says "posterior," but I'm not through with him yet.

"Mr. Shelton. You reading my booty? Is that what this is all about? You reading *h-o-t c-h-i-c-k* on my ass?"

"Go to class, young lady."

"I'm going, Mr. Shelton. I'm going. Don't forget to check out my artwork in C Corridor. Black History Month," I say. "See, Mr. Shelton. You made me late. I'm going to miss the polypeptides and fail the quiz but I'll have an alibi. I'll tell Miss Womack I was showing Shel-E-Shel my outfit." I do my shaky-shake and keep it shaking down the hall. I know he's laughing, trying to look serious, but why turn around and bust him? I brighten his day. He'll smile from now until 2:45. Why? Because that's what I do. Bring a little joy to someone's drab, dull day. That's right. I bring color to this school.

6
Social Interaction

DOMINIQUE

UNH-UNH. Can't let her cut into me like that. Through my space. Through me. Can't let that slide. She has to know, she can't do that.

What? She didn't see me? Do I look invisible to you? *Do I?*

I can't let it slide. Can't let it slide.

It's all right. I'll handle it. Handle it. Set her straight. She'll learn.

" 'Nique, are you all right?"

"Yeah." I'm not but I'm cool for now and take my seat.

Fenster, boy. She's always watching. Even when she's teaching, she's watching.

Social Interaction is for kids with problems. Kids who don't know how to act. Kids with stuff going on. Kids who need to be watched.

I'm not one of them.

They think I am. Say I am. Have it on my record: watch Dominique Duncan. She's got problems. A temper. Put her in Social Interaction for life. Block that shot.

Fenster's got these posters up on both sides of the classroom. Ten rules for Social Interaction. I can see them. All ten. I read them every class. They're in my face. I can't *not* read them. I understand what they're saying. I get the rules. They're just not my rules. My rules make sense:

I'm not in your face, don't be in mine. It's when you mess with my stuff—my minutes, my space, my girls, my guy, my peace of mind—that I have to respond. Correct you. Let you know you can't do that. Mess with my stuff, my people, my frame of mind. My rules are simple. Don't mess with me, I don't mess with you. I'm a yard with a big-ass sign: DO NOT TRESPASS. It's that simple.

If you don't like me, that's fine. Just keep your Dominique-hating self on your side of the lane. Then we don't have problems. No contact, no foul. Simple. You see me coming down B, find A. Just don't rub up against me. Don't say my name. Don't point when you're with your girls. Not with your fingers, not with your eyes. Don't whisper, don't laugh. Don't Dominique nothing.

See, I don't have a temper. A temper's like having freckles or being bowlegged. A person with a temper is set off by anything. But I don't have a temper. I'm not what they say. What they write. I'm not a problem child.

I just care about my stuff. Take a shot at me or to me and I block it. It's reflex. Instinct. Natural. I just don't back down. And it—*BOOM!*—happens quick. That's different from having a temper. A dog has a temper, hear what I'm saying? *Stay away from that pit bull because that dog's foaming for no reason.* I'm not like that. I don't bother no one. I don't. I'm all peace. Just leave me alone, all right? Read the sign in the yard.

Go ahead. Say what you want to say about me and let me catch you. You better mean what you say like it's word. Do what you want to do. Take what you want to take from me. Take it like it's yours. You better be happy with it because I won't let it slide when I respond. That's not a temper. That's me responding. Correcting. Setting things straight.

Response is up there on Fenster's posters. Appropriate response. Inappropriate response. I apply that to my rules. If you come out inappropriate, I come back, appropriate. One takes care of the other.

If anyone needs Social Interaction it's those girls from last year. Do they still go here? Anyway, they should be taking notes on how to get along. They came out inappropriate, not me. They shouldn't have been in my face. They were sophomores and I just got here. They should have had better things to do than to be talking about my jersey, my sneakers. Oh, right. I'm supposed to stand there like a big dumb bitch and pretend I don't hear them speak my name? I'm supposed to walk by like it's all right for them to laugh at me? I'm supposed to be their joke? Their girlie gossip of the day? Well, they opened their mouths and I responded. Corrected them. Simple as that. But when the dust cleared, no one saw three against one. They just saw the one still standing and three down.

"Come on, 'Nique. Let's go, let's go, let's go!" Fenster is like Coach blowing the whistle during laps. Let's go. Get those knees up.

I'm all right with Fenster and she's all right with me. She gave me an 80 last term. She's not trying to hold me back. Keep me sidelined. She knows I need those points.

After the suspension last year, they sent me to her and she worked out the plea bargain: "Dominique has skills on the court. A team sport will help her interact socially and learn to cooperate with others." That's also on the poster. Cooperation.

AP Shelton said two conditions: "Social Interaction and keep a clean nose for the next three years."

Coach said, "Keep your grades up, do what I tell you, and you'll be starting at guard by junior year."

I go along with it. I do my time. As long as I can be on the team. Get some minutes on the court. So two days a week, I got SI. Freshman, sophomore, junior, senior, SI. Rules for Social Interaction. Surrounded by kids with real problems, real stories about their real problems. Sick-ass stories. After each one, Fenster asks, "What did you learn?" and "How is this different from the last time?" Me? I don't have no stories. So don't ask me what I learned. But I show up. I'm here. I hold up my end of the deal.

The Do Now is to come up with three priorities.

"Not everything is a level-one priority," Fenster says.

That's what we're learning. How to prioritize, figure out what's important. How to stack them in order of importance.

I got my three and I arrange them in order. What I'll say is most important and what I'll say is least important. So, when Fenster asks me why aren't I writing, I point to my head and say, "It's up here."

"Okay, 'Nique. Let's hear them." Fenster tests me

because she doubts me. That's her thing. *I've been around. I'm wise to the game.*

That's cool. I'm ready. I say, "Get back my minutes on the court." That's number one. Level one.

She nods and holds up one finger.

"Up my grades." Yeah. I'm gonna squeeze that little brown mouse when I get up to the third floor.

She nods, two fingers. Big smile. I'm getting a "plus" in the book of pluses and minuses. That's how she scores us. Too many minuses and we get a one-on-one. The intervention.

"Improve my D" is the last one I give her. The fake-out. She should know better but holds up a third finger. She should know improving my defense is like breathing or eating. Everyday stuff. See, the real priority is as important as the first. Dealing with the third priority last doesn't make it a level-three priority. It's just the order that it will go down in, at 2:45. It's a top priority. A personal priority. It's not that I *want* to respond to it, I *have* to respond to it. I can't let that slide.

7

Imaginary or Not

LETICIA

CLASS IS IN FULL SWING WHEN I ARRIVE. Mr. Walsh doesn't bother to ask for the late pass. It's not the first time I've strolled in after the second bell. He figures, Why waste valuable class time asking for a pass he knows I don't have? So I shock him, uncrumple the bathroom pass with Miss Palenka's signature and smooth it out on his desk so he can see it's legitimate.

"A long bathroom break, Miss Moore."

"A long dump, Mr. Walsh."

Now isn't he sorry? He upset his morning coffee and McBiscuit commenting when he should have nodded and kept teaching. A lesson for you, Mr. Walsh. Stick with your classics. Stick with what you know.

I sashay s-l-o-w because I want to freeze the moment for him like we're on a TV show where the funny black girl puts a cap on the scene. I take my seat, dig out *A Separate Peace*, a sheet of paper, and a pen.

You know, life is unfair. Bea's class has *Push* and *I Know Why the Caged Bird Sings* for winter-break reading. They're reading true-to-life dramas. Stuff that makes your eyes run right, left, right like feet on fire. Our class has *Black Boy*, *The Stranger*, and Mr. Walsh's favorite, *A Separate Peace*. "A book every high school student must read," according to Walsh. I see his point. One day I might transfer to an elite military school, befriend a bunch of losers, climb a tree, and watch a classmate fall and break his leg. That's right. Pushed or fell, the classmate breaks a leg and dies. He doesn't die on the spot. Dying drags out over time so the so-called friend can Hamletize over to tell or not to tell that he's responsible for the broken leg and his classmate's death. So yeah. I see how it all relates to my life because every other day I'm up a tree pushing some loser to his eventual death, then breaking out into a soliloquy. Don't you just love the classics?

I read the book. Every page, even when I wanted to skim. I already have zero-period math. I don't need to rise at an ungodly hour for zero-period English next semester.

I look around. Unlike everyone else's book, mine is brand-new, no cracks, no creases down the spine. Each page corner as sharp as when I bought it. Not a highlighter or pen mark to be found between the covers. You can't get your money back from the store if it looks used. It's not easy to read a book you don't crack open all the way, but I've mastered the art of keeping the book brand-new. *Black Boy*, *The Stranger*, and *A Separate Peace* are all crisp and clean. Ready to be returned along with the receipt.

Can't say that about Bea's books. Both *Push* and *Caged Bird* been through the war with Bea. Their spines broken, their covers like arms forced back in surrender. "Ease up, Bea. Don't hurt a book," I'd say, trying to grab her attention. It didn't do any good. I lost Bea for two weeks during her *Push*, *Caged Bird* phase. She read both books twice. First time was for class; the second, she said, was for her. And that was all she wanted to talk about. Marguerite this, Precious that. I would have read her novels too if I could have gotten credit for it. Instead I had my hands full with *Black Boy*, *The Stranger*, and *A Separate Peace*. The sophomore classics.

"And what do you suppose 'Maginot Lines' refers to at the end of the novel?"

I can't be mad at Mr. Walsh. He can't help himself. He loves English. Look at how he throws out questions, like a pitcher eager to throw the first pitch of the season. He's like Bea, all filled up with a book and can't wait to talk about it. If Bea read her books twice, Mr. Walsh read his twenty times. Come on, now. Only paste is whiter than Mr. Walsh's face. You know that's what he does all day. Stays indoors and reads his classics. And now he's bursting. Bursting like we're an honors class and we're all fighting each other to talk about Gene and Finny and Leper and Quackenbush.

I throw my hand up. I usually hang back, but if I answer his question now, I can spend the rest of the class taking notes uncalled on. Minimum effort goes a long way, which is where I went wrong with Mr. Jiang last semester. I didn't go up to the board or raise my hand at least once a day to give that one answer I knew. Had I done that, Jiang would have scraped up thirteen points for me. But it's all right. I have my hand up now because I plan to sleep late next semester.

Just hold it together, Mr. Walsh. Don't be like Mr. Yerkewicz, having a heart attack in the middle of class. Don't let the sight of my hand waving in the air hit you, because that would make two shocks in a row. A legitimate bathroom pass and an answer from Leticia, not five minutes apart.

"Yes, Leticia. Maginot Lines."

So what if he says Magino and I read Maginot with the full *not*. I swear, the French language is there to trip you up. Silent *t*'s and *x*'s and *l*'s. Every class I go, there is French, making trouble. I focus on "Maginot Lines" and minimum effort. I'll deal with French later.

I say, " 'Maginot Lines' either means imaginary lines or not imaginary lines. It depends how you look at it." I could have Googled it like the syllabus suggested but *Maginot* is one of those words you don't have to look up because it sounds like its meaning even if it's spelled inside out. Dang French. I'm positive "imaginary" is the English translation of *Maginot*. It sounds right.

Mr. Walsh rocks back and forth in his brown teacher's snow shoes. "Hmm. Imaginary lines," he sings, ponders, nods, and says, "Or not imaginary lines. Okay. Let's go with imaginary lines. That's a good place to start."

I nod also. It wasn't on the money but it wasn't wrong. He didn't say, "Shut the hell up, Miss Moore, sashaying into my class with your 'imaginary lines or not.' " He didn't cap the scene in our TV show while the audience laughed in the background.

I can relax. I've done my job for the day. I got the discussion rolling and Mr. Walsh even uses "imaginary lines" in his next question. Turns out Lorna and half the class Googled "Maginot Lines." She starts out, "Like

Leticia was saying"—already I like Lorna, Jamaican girl with her "tick" accent, talking about how the French set up imaginary lines of defense to protect themselves from the Germans. That's right, Lorna. Show some unity. Show some solidarity. Don't make my answer wrong.

Herman couldn't wait to announce that it was in our global history book. He actually lugged that seven-pound (I weighed it) textbook into class just to show the cartoon of greedy Germany camped out on the borders of France, salivating. I'm copying notes, so I can't plaster a proper L for "big loser" against my forehead for Herman's benefit.

I almost ask Mr. Walsh what does Germany ganging up on poor little France have to do with Gene and Finny and Leper and Quackenbush, but I've already done my part. I got the ball rolling. Besides. Look at Mr. Walsh's pale white face. He can't wait to tell us.

8

Polypeptide Jam

TRINA

"HONEST, MISS WOMACK. I don't mean to be late. I'm handing in my gorgeous artwork to Mr. Sebastian for Black History Month—check it out. C Corridor. And while I'm rushing to get here, AP Shelton stops me in the hall. We had a discussion. You know AP Shelton. He loves chatting with me."

I don't know why she casts those blue flecks of doubt at me but she does.

"Serious, Miss W. I have an alibi. Check with the AP."

I slide down in my seat. The metal bottom is cold so I shimmy it warm and pull out my colored pens and my Biology notebook. I take the scenic route through pages of diagrams in my fully color-coordinated notebook. Apple green, baby blue, maroon, hot pink, *naranja* for the diagrams, Bic black for the info. Soft brown for the first diagram, the monkey-to-man page. (Can't show that to Mami—it upsets her.) Apple greens, deep greens for the plant world. Maroons, hot pinks, and dark blue for the molecules. Get back, *Picassa!* I air-kiss a perfect water molecule, wet smack.

Me? Settle down? Am I disturbing things?

"Sorry, Miss Womack." The pages flapping, the chair legs rocking, all mess with her teaching flow. She gets really bothered when she's interrupted, so I quickly find the right spot in my notebook. A blank page, ready for more Cell World.

I write, *Subject: Polypeptides and Proteins*, then *Today's Aim: Forming Bonds*. Dang! Miss Womack has the full diagram up already. Five minutes with AP Shelton cost me a choice of greens, blues, *naranja* (which sounds better, orange or *naranja? Naranja*, right? Prettier). No color coordinating. Just go for it. Catch up. Dang, Miss Womack talks fast.

I lean toward Eduardo's paper to see what's been said so far. I'm his leafy plant, leaning to his open notebook like it's the warm gold sun. Eduardo leans away, digging the plant biology. He inches his notebook to the right, coaxing, *Trina, lean closer, my way. Closer.* We both think, *Anything for a peek.* Only, I want the cell words, he wants more Trina. I smile but Eduardo fakes being undercover.

Doesn't matter how old they are—fifty-five or fifteen. They can be so shy. I completely make his day.

Word for word, I copy everything on Eduardo's page. What they are, what they mean, and what they do. Whatever I don't know I'll look up later. For now, I'm done with Eduardo and flip my lovely locks as I face front. Eduardo can live on what I just gave him until the end of semester.

I still want to make my page pretty. I want to get the diagram as good as I can. So what if I can't coordinate like I want to. I can fix it up later.

With the maroon, I draw the big bean, the nucleus. Blue spaghetti strands wrapped with *naranja*, looping like a jump rope in full swing, the wrapping and twining. Bic black for transcription, translation—what?—no matter. I'll catch it later.

I giggle when I get to the ribosome. What? You can't see what she has on the board? I think I'm giggling to myself but—

"*Trina.*"

Again. "Sorry, miss."

Okay, Trina. Chill.

I mean to listen and write but I can't keep still. I peek

over at Eduardo's diagram. Then over to Nilda, on my left, but Nilda is giving me back a glare, so whatever. I don't dare turn to Krystal, behind me. Miss Womack is bothered enough as it is. Between Eduardo and Al'liah, I'm not the only one to see Miss Womack has drawn a lopsided, goose-bumped boy sac under the bean. The DNA ribbon runs between the big one and the small one but that doesn't disguise a thing. I draw my boy sacs like Miss Womack's, the upper one bigger than the lower. I laugh to myself. Ding, dong, dang, boy. How's it hanging?

"Problem, Trina?"

I can't believe everyone holds their faces together. Don't they want to bust out?

"Nothing, miss. I'm just drawing." I give her innocence. Nothing but innocence. What?

Miss Womack revs up. She talks really fast, yo! Her words race together but you hear each one crisp and clear. So fast, so crisp and clear, I want to dance to the quickness. It's like a jam. The peptide jam. Then a polypeptide jam. With the polypeptide bond. Check out how fast she spits that: amino acids, proteins, polypeptide bonds. Miss W dates a DJ, for sure. They flip syllables back and forth, fast, fast, fast. I'm picturing it right now.

When she takes a breather, I jump on the pause and raise my hand to ask a question. Smirks all around. They think I'm going to ask about the lumpy boy sac but I'm over that. I surprise them all.

"How do they know?" I ask instead.

"Excuse me?"

That's what people say when they need a moment to pull it together, but Miss Womack is a brain. You can't stump the star, so I say it again on the chance she truly missed my question.

"How do they know, Miss W? How do they know what to do? Where to go? Every little piece breaks down to smaller and smaller pieces. Every little piece is something, does something. And those pieces get together and do it."

It's the way I said "do it" that has the class laughing. But can you imagine? Cells, nucleus, strings, strands, all inside us, doing it. Chatting, hooking up, Xeroxing all the little pieces, making new pieces, making bonds. Isn't that amazing? Polypeptides bond. Amino acids bond. Even water molecules bond. All those little pieces, smaller than a speck of sand, and they know what to do and they just roll with the flow. They do it.

9

All About the Angle

LETICIA

DO YOU SEE WHAT I SEE? I cannot believe my eyes. And no shame or apology whatsoever!

Mr. Jiang whips out his credit-card-thin cell phone and takes a call in class. He is outright taunting me, like, *This is a real phone and that fat little girl in your bag needs to diet.*

To borrow one of those teacher sayings, I am appalled. I find his classroom behavior appalling and outrageous and I won't stand for it. I have to speak up.

"The No Cell Phone rule applies to you too, Mr. Jiang."

He says, "The work on the board applies to you," turns his back, and chats away, leaving the class to "Oh, snap!" and "Ah-hah" all around me.

* * *

Mr. Jiang has every triangle known to man on the board. Right, obtuse, acute, complementary, perpendicular, along with a list of givens. All I have to do is copy them down, but instead of writing "Given: an equilateral triangle is a triangle with all sides equal," I write, "Given: Bea has more crust than Wonder Bread. A whole loaf of crust."

I can't believe her. *You gotta tell her, Leticia.*

Just because you thought you saw something doesn't mean you actually saw what you thought you saw. No one knows this better than Bea.

Last semester, she and I were riding the bus, on our way to the MAC counter at Macy's for makeovers. Call it kismet, but both Bea and I looked out the window in time to see Jay and Krystal standing at the corner face on face. Now, the bus was rolling fast, and we caught them at a funny angle, but that was Jay and that was Krystal and they were closer than they should have been. Bea and Jay been going out since freshman year, so she can spot his face in a grainy four-by-six double-exposed photo with fifty other faces in it. Bea knows her Jay.

We rang the bell, jumped off the bus, headed straight toward Jay and Krystal. So what if we wasted a fare. Watching Bea catch Jay with his hand in the cookie jar was worth the lost bus fare and half the lip gloss at the

MAC counter. Dirt didn't get any better than this and I had the best seat in the house.

We were a block away and they saw us. Jay's head jerked. Then Krystal was backing away.

Bea—picture this, right, because Bea's no little girl. She's packed like I am. So Bea was trotting up to Krystal and then Jay jumped in front of her and said, "It's not what you think, Bea. It's not what you think."

"What did I see, Jay? Tell me, what did I just see?" Krystal was down the block but in Bea's mind she was an inch away so Bea was going after her. Krystal was rocking those new fall boots with the cute heels. Cowboy-style but skinny. Like stiletto but not quite. Anyway, you're not supposed to run in those joints but Krystal was tearing up the sidewalk.

Jay was still saying "It's not what you think and you didn't see what you thought you saw." Question: How many times can a guy say that before he starts to say something else? Thirteen times. Lucky thirteen! Bea weaved from side to side trying to get around Jay, and Jay kept saying "It's not what you think," all the while blocking her path so she couldn't go after Krystal. "You didn't see what you thought you saw."

Me? I was just there collecting every word for the playback. I was enjoying my front-row seat.

On the fourteenth try, the needle on the record broke. Jay said he bent down to tell Krystal something and we must have seen them at that precise moment, that precise angle. He said it's all in where you're standing or riding by. It's all about the angle.

Jiang never made angles sound this good. If he had, I would have popped back with a snappy "given" topped off with a "therefore." Unfortunately I didn't know jack about angles and said nothing.

Jay was doing it. Working his game on Bea. Her body held tight but her eyes gave in. I was glued to the TV set, like, *damn*. I couldn't believe it was playing out like this. Jay rapped a side-angle-side talk and Bea gave in. What a letdown. And I was anticipating a show with Bea going buck wild for a change, and it wasn't going to happen.

Think, Leticia, think, I told myself. Bea's your girl and you have the best seat in the house. And then it came to me. Just before Jay sighed his dodged-the-bullet sigh of relief, I asked, "So, Jay. What did you have to tell Krystal you had to be in her lip gloss?"

Pay dirt! Jay was not loving me at that moment. "Mind your business, Leticia, and let me mind mine." He pointed to him and Bea and said, "This is between me and she. You are outside the equation."

"Brackets, Jay? That's algebra. That's last year. We're

talking about this year. This day. Explain the geometry, Jay. You know. The triangle. Go on." All that was missing was the guy who yells, "Cut! That's a wrap! Good job, Miss Moore."

Bea sprang back to life. "Tell me what you were telling Krystal, 'cause I'm going to find out."

Still, I stepped back, pretending to give them privacy, but it was a small step back. My front-row seat was too good to give up completely.

Maybe Jay cared about Bea or maybe he was just rapping as a reflex: deny all accusations, even if caught red-handed. Maybe it was a little of both. It's definitely a guy thing. Got to keep his cake but must have some cookies on the side. But don't let another guy glance Bea's way. Jay is on the scene, visible, hovering, playing the boyfriend role for the Academy Award. He may want his chocolate-chip cookies in his pocket but he's not giving up that rich chocolate cake on his plate.

Anyway, he could have come clean and said, "Bea, you and me's been forever but it's just time to move on. . . ." Nope. Jay was rapping his heart out like he was about to be signed to a record label.

"First, I'm up here," he said. "Krystal's down there."

We gave him the "Yeah." And it's true. Jay's tall.

"Eddie likes Krystal but Eddie's too shy, y'know. I

was just greasing it as a favor to Eddie. But everything I said, Krystal kept saying 'Huh? Huh?' And I had to keep repeating myself so I bent down. And when y'all saw us, I was at her ear at that moment telling her for Eddie. Come on. You know Eddie. Ask him. Call him now and ask him. It's just that what you thought you saw wasn't that at all. You just caught it at the wrong angle at the wrong time so it looked like something it wasn't."

Now, if Bea went for that, why's she so sure I saw what I thought I saw? I could have been wrong. I could have been seeing it from the wrong angle. Just because Dominique looked like she was going to kick Trina's ass doesn't mean that's exactly what I saw. And this is my point. Why would I get involved in Trina's life when I don't know for sure if I saw what I thought I saw? Who is to say that Dominique doesn't mean something else? Who is to say I wasn't seeing it from the wrong angle?

10

Think Cold War Russia

DOMINIQUE

"COME ALIVE, CLASS. COME ALIVE."

Delmonico's funny, man. Flapping his arms like a duck or a chicken.

"Cold War, remember? You read about it last night. Come on, folks. Get with it."

The class draws a collective blank. That doesn't stop Delmonico. Those arms are flapping. If we believed he could fly we'd start talking about the Cold War.

"Just because they fought a common foe doesn't mean—" He scopes the room for a hand. "What?" Still scoping. "What?"

I get it but I don't answer. I don't volunteer. My hands stay in my lap and I lean back in my chair. Getting it is enough. Enough for the surprise quiz. It's never a surprise. Delmonico flips that comb-over, winks, and says, "Study extrahard tonight."

He's desperate. *Throw me a rope. Anybody. Anything.* Eyebrows on both sides of his head slant upward like praying hands.

I couldn't be him. Poor bastard. Beg when no one wants to be bothered. But that's his job. Give a damn when we don't. When we won't show it. Keep coming up with the lesson, the plays. Keep talking it, writing it, quizzing it. And he does. Got to give it to him, poor bastard. He shows up. Suited. Ready. This is his game. His minutes. It's gotta suck when you're the only one ready on game day.

So I call out, "Trust. It doesn't mean they trust each other."

Delmonico's so grateful for the full chest pass. "You're on it, 'Nique," he says, and he's crazy excited. "You're right on it."

Imagine this is your game. This is what you live for. He's got the ball and now he wants to pass it. He's looking out at the players. Who has the hot hand? Who's open?

"Come on, people. Come on. Why don't they trust each other?"

And there's no one to pass it to. He's dribbling, dribbling, keeping one eye on the ball.

"Lucia."

Lucia sucks her tongue in her mouth. A hard you-make-me-sick suck.

"You're marrying Omar this Saturday," Delmonico says.

This has nowhere to go. Nowhere to go but silly. The guys all woof like big dogs to say Omar's a lucky dude. Lucia says she'll kill herself first. But look at her. She's soaking it up.

The ball's about to drop out of Delmonico's hands. He's about to lose control but he pushes through. Like he doesn't hear her begging him to choose a different guy to marry. He raises his voice, talking over her whining. "Your mother meets his mother to plan the wedding but it doesn't go well. They can't agree on anything."

She says of course they can't agree. Her mother doesn't speak whatever Omar's mother speaks.

"Exactly! So how do they communicate?"

"Interpreters."

"Telepathy."

"Smoke signals."

"They DM each other."

"And text."

"Wedding's off."

Delmonico doesn't care how stupid it gets in here. As long as we're with him. He can deal with stupid. He pushes through it.

"Let's go back to what Dominique said." He winks my way. "Why don't they trust each other to make the right plans for the wedding?" Blanks all around. "Come on, folks. Look alive. Same reason why Lucia's mother and Omar's mother can't agree."

I get it. I get Russia. I feed him another. "They don't speak the same language, so they don't understand each other."

He, like, has it near the basket and wants to sink two easy.

"Chances are, they have what in common?" He pivots. *Anyone? Anyone?*

Another player steps up from the bench. "Nothing."

"Bingo! They have *what* in common? They have nothing in common." Delmonico's wild for that one little "nothing." He's excited and has too much head action. That comb-over's flipping like crazy. He's writing out the players and the plays. Three O's and one giant X. The thirty-second clock is winding down and he can run away with this. "Now let's look at the USSR, the US, France, and England. Starting with economies. How are they different?"

More players step up from the bench. Delmonico's hearing the crowd go wild for the buzzer beater. He's teaching his teacher heart out. He's funny as hell to watch but I get it. He just wants to play his full game.

"And if we're in class in Cold War Russia, what are you studying? Here's a hint: it isn't Shakespeare and it isn't Music Appreciation. Come on, people. Think Cold War Russia." And he's winking on "War."

Then that simple flit Lucia says, "You mean that's it? No more wedding?"

Omar tells her it's okay. Don't cry. He still wants her. Lucia's mouth is full of sucking sounds and "You wishes."

I don't bother to throw her a look. She irritates me. Yeah. She's an irritant. Irritating simple flit.

Not everyone is meant to get along. Not everyone should be in each other's faces. Fenster doesn't say that in SI but it should be up there on her list. I don't have nothing in common with girls like Lucia. Girls like that. It's all an act: *Pick me but don't pick me. Get away from me but come here.* A bitch should be clear, you know. She should say what she means and mean what she says.

I'm clear.

I'm not confused.

I don't act.

I don't play cute.

I know what I want. I have my priorities. My rules.
You can trust me to mean what I say, do what I say.
I don't give off crossed signals. No smoke signals.
I don't make confusion. I keep it clear.

11

Honking Like a Goose

LETICIA

"NO, NO, LETEESEEYA. Do not pronounce the *s*.

"No, no, Leteeseeya. Do not pronounce the *t*.

"No, no, Leteeseeya. Say *aun, aun, aun*. Feel it! Way back in the throat and out of the nose. Not *anh*. *Aun!*

"Repeat after me, Leteeseeya: *aun, aun, aun*."

I can't believe it. I can't believe it. Madame LeCoeur has me honking like a goose in the middle of this classroom.

"These vowels are too hard, Madame LeCoeur."

She scrunches her nose, hating the way I say her name.

"LeCoeur. *Oer*, like *courage*. Not like liquor store."

"Okay," I say. "Then I want Leticia, like Leticia, not like Leteeseeya. That's three syllables—like, one, two, three—so we're even."

I was hoping that was enough for her to be fed up and transfer me out of her class. Instead she goes back to the vowels and says, "We use everything for the French language: lungs, nose, lips, tongue, teeth, throat. Everything. You have to feel this deep, Leteeseeya. You have to work hard for this. Again. *Aun, aun, aun.*"

Her bony hands are on my throat and I can't believe this is happening. Minimum effort doesn't work with Madame LeCoeur. Giving my one answer turns into another episode of "No, no, Leteeseeya." Madame LeCoeur is supposed to say, "*Merci*, Mademoiselle Leteeseeya. Sit back and take notes, Mademoiselle Leteeseeya." Not "Sit here and honk like a goose." The Haitians in the class are all tuned in to the show. They're all cracking up and speaking Creole, which makes Madame LeCoeur call out, "Silence, *s'il vous plaît!*"

If the sophomore band can play "What a Wonderful World" with the clarinets squeaking and the trumpets blasting out of tune, why can't I get through these vowels the best way I know how? Why do I have to be singled out, all eyes on Leticia? Why must French be so hard?

It's not my fault Spanish is overcrowded and Señora Roberts doesn't want one more face to look at. It's not my fault I didn't fix my schedule when I got it in the mail. By the time I opened it, the deadline for changes had passed and there was nothing I could do. Honestly I thought it was the usual "Here's your class schedule, Leticia. Good to go" letter. How was I supposed to know it said, "Look here, Miss Leticia Moore. If you want Spanish, you better speak up. And by the way, you know you have to repeat geometry, right? You know you failed, right? You know you got to get here forty-five minutes early while everyone else squeezes the last five minutes out the snooze alarm. You know you gotta sit with Miss Palenka and the rest of the repeaters."

Well, I have a solution to this entire situation. Take the Puerto Rican kids, the Dominicans, the Mexicans, the Colombians, and the Ecuadorians out of Spanish and give them two periods of English as their foreign language. They don't need more Spanish. They *hablan con mucho gusto* already.

I took Spanish I and II. I can conjugate the *ar* and the *er* verbs. I can answer in the positive and in the negative, in the present and past tenses. I can roll the double *r*'s and halfway work that tilde. I can break out what they saying at the corner bodega when I pass by. *Fat ass* sounds the same in every language. It's how they say it. Since they like that fat ass, I know they're saying it in a good way. I have a shot at not only passing Spanish but of getting an 80 or higher as long as it doesn't get too tricky.

Let's face it. French isn't anything but a trick. Not one word is said the way it's spelled, or you have to dig way back into your throat or your nose to say it. That's why the French were afraid of the Germans. They knew the Germans were coming to change their language. Have you heard German? *Achtung*, baby. Sounds rough, right? Not that I'd want to take German, but I can see why Germany was through with France. France thought she was cute with all her invisible consonants and invisible lines, and Germany was trying to keep things real.

12

Write Naked

TRINA

I LIKE THIS CLASS.

I like Ms. Bauer.

I like how we usually start with journal entries before we open *The Grapes of Wrath*.

This morning I'm not liking this class so much. For the first time, I draw a blank. Blank page. Blank me. It doesn't happen often. In fact, it happens never, so I don't know how to be. Silent. Still. Waiting. *Nada.* Blank. Damn.

It is strictly hot-pink ink for the journal entries. My pen is used to rolling across the sheet, right, back to left, right, back to left, moving so fast the tip stays kissing the paper with no letup, no liftoff while I race to the clinker. The closer. The winner. Whatever they call the last line that's so good it makes the room holler "*Oh, shnikies*"

when you want to say, "Oh, shit," or makes you say, "*Deep*"
for "double damn." No curses in Ms. Bauer's class. She
says, "There's too many words to only use the same lazy
three." Ms. Bauer keeps a bar of soap for dirty mouths in
her desk—*what?*—that's for real.

I always speed write, rolling along the lines, breathing fast, smiling to myself because my journals are funny
and the class is dying to hear me read. Ramón, Josh,
Devlin, and them chant "Tree-na, Tree-na" when they
catch me writing and giggling. I never disappoint. It's
always the "Oh, shnikies." Never "That's deep," like when
Nilda reads from her journal.

Today the topic on the board is "With _____ I
am complete."

In case you don't know, Ms. Bauer is a Ms. She'll
tell you straight up: "Mizzz Bauer." Don't say Miss, Mrs.,
or Ma—like you don't call your favorite teacher or your
mean teacher Ma. You know you do.

Ms. Bauer smiles at the confusion on our faces. Ma
says, "Fill the blank line with an item or a personal attri-
bute, like a sense of humor if a sense of humor makes you
complete. Maybe it's a person or pet." She tells us to write
without stopping. Write without caring. Write naked.

Who wouldn't laugh at that? Even though Ma got a
barbwire tattoo around her wrist and green soap in her

top drawer, nobody is writing. Everyone's riffing on writing naked. Ramón tells Michael and Devlin to put on some clothes. Devlin says, "Trina, you heard: write naked." But it's not just me they say it to. Before you know it all the boys are telling all the girls, "Get writing. Get stripped." Except Nilda. Something must have happened to Nilda because she is like a dead saint and you respect dead saints. Ramón and them don't say "Write naked" to her.

Ms. Bauer is used to us. She doesn't panic, slam the textbook against her desk, or take out the soap. She holds up her right hand and says, "Pens up," which means "Get serious."

All silliness stops. Twenty-two hands find pens. A few kids still dig for pens or beg to borrow. I roll my hot-pink pen against my lucky gold chain, waiting for a thought to come.

When we are serious, ready, Ms. Bauer says, "This is private writing." That means we keep it to ourselves. No sharing. For me that means no "Oh, shnikies."

Five minutes is all the time in the world to spill out what makes Trina the full, completed Trina. Or does she mean if I had fill-in-the-blank I would be complete? I just sit quiet. I stay blank.

When the class is quiet like that, you hear everything. Hard breathing. The clock ticking. It's weird.

Start with the heading. Name, class, and date. I write the title. "With _____ I am complete."

Although I'm sitting still, there is crazy scribbling around me. I hear the pens tearing up paper. Lines of looping, crossing, dotting. They're off and running like skinny greyhounds gunning the racetrack. They are writing naked.

I play with my lucky gold chain and I remember how lucky I am. That I have talent pouring out of me and I'm always showing them, sharing them. I know why I'm not writing naked: My life is good. I am complete. I don't wake up wishing I had clothes and money. What I have is good. I don't say, "I need more this and I'll be set." What I have works. I don't want green eyes, blue eyes, hazel eyes. These light brown eyes set me off just right in Picasso perfection—except my eyes aren't painted on my tatas; they're where they belong. It's about the perfection. I'm like art.

I don't look at someone's shoes and say, "I want those." I don't see Malik, the darkest of dark chocolate, all smiles and muscles—*what?*—hugging Natalie and be jealous. Even when Malik licks his lips at me, I don't start drawing our names together and plotting for him. I know what's up. If Malik and I are supposed to be hugged up down B Corridor we'll get to that. But I don't have that hunger like I have to break open the Mounds bar to get to that coconutty smile. I can't say biting into that would make me complete.

There's no things—no pets, no person—to make me complete. Just Mami. For a little woman Mami is big like a blanket. What? Can I breathe with all that Mami wrapped around me?

When I'm racked up sick and have to stay home with her, we laugh at those stupid women who are 1,000 percent sure that Jerome/Julio/Jethro is the baby's daddy, only to have their faces cracked on live TV, ten million people watching. Keisha/CoCo/Kaitlyn still brings her business to the people and now Jerome/Julio/Jethro's mama is doing her dance around Keisha/CoCo/Kaitlyn's body, wagging her finger while Jerome/Julio/Jethro raises his hands like he's gone platinum at the Garden and Keisha/CoCo/Kaitlyn is down on the ground kicking and crying buckets and saying "I'm so sorry . . ." because you can't deny the DNA.

And after Mami and I have our laugh she feels under my chin and says, "*Bueno*. Getting better."

But she still doesn't tell you who your father is and what he is.

You still don't know how your own DNA coil is wrapped. You still don't know zip about that missing part of you or where he is.

Mami says he isn't important. And when you see yourself in the mirror and you look good and you have everything going for you, you know she is right. Whoever he is, wherever he is, at least he gave you the best parts.

Then I start to giggle. Two minutes left and the hot-pink ink is rolling. "Can you imagine not looking like this? Not being like this? No. I'm complete. Life is good." I make sure I write that: *Life is good.*

13

Get Involved

LETICIA

THE P.A. CRACKLING FIVE MINUTES into homeroom means one thing, and the whole class, including Mr. Adelman, knows it. Jessie and Turtle are already out of their seats to dance to fifteen seconds of "Get Up, Get into It, Get Involved." It's still too early in the day to hear James Brown screaming at you, telling you what you're supposed to do. And it's never the right time to hear Principal Bates coming in on the scream, telling you to be a solid school citizen, show school spirit, and get involved with service activities. Principal Bates is full of ideas on getting our attention, getting attendance up, and getting test scores up. Bridgette and Bernie love Principal Bates's enthusiasm. I wouldn't be surprised if that's Bridgette and Bernie's *The Very Best of James Brown* CD on loan, screaming through the P.A.

Even though the music plays for fifteen seconds, you know it's JB. You can't just shake JB out of your head. From now until the 2:45 bell rings I'll hear JB, the hardest-working man in show bidness—according to Bridgette and Bernie—tell me to get up, get into it, get involved. The school shouldn't be allowed to do that. Mess with your subconscious. Anyway, if my mind goes blank for more than five seconds and I want to daydream about Chem II James, JB is sure to grab the mike, the one right next to my brain's ear, and holler, "Leticia! Get up, get into it, get involved, get involved."

What Principal Bates should do is find a song called "Mind Your Business." If people minded their business everything would be straight. Contrary to popular opinion, "minding your business" is a misunderstood term. To mind your business is a good thing. A smart thing. More people should do just that. But tell someone to mind their business and they get hot. Instead, if you listen to what's being said, your response should be "Thank you" when someone says mind your business. They're just freeing your mind. It isn't your concern. You don't have to worry about it. Go on about your business.

Leticia Corinthia Moore is all about her own business. If it concerns Leticia, then Leticia becomes the fact finder. Why? It's a fact about Leticia and therefore it's

Leticia's business to know. And by the way, Bea concerns Leticia, so Jay telling Leticia to mind her own business is void and nullified because what concerns Bea concerns Leticia and vice versa.

Now, what is on Dominique's mind is none of Leticia's business. So if I, Leticia, tap Dominique's broad shoulders and say, "What's going on between you and Trina?" and she says, "Mind your business," she would be in the right, and I would be in the wrong. Why? Because what's going on between Dominique and Trina don't have anything to do with Leticia Corinthia Moore. It's a Dominique-Trina line, not a Dominique-Trina-Leticia triangle. Why? Because I'm not in it. It's not my business. Therefore, I stay out of it. But if I pull Trina's coat and say, "Trina. You know Dominique?" Trina will a) rustle up what crew she can get, b) cut out and run after lunch, or most likely c) confront Dominique and say, "Leticia said . . ."

See, it's those two words, *Leticia said,* that cause problems. Because what should Leticia have done in the first place? Minded her own business. Half the turmoil brewing happens because so-and-so didn't do what? Mind her business.

When you get down to it, we don't even know what's on Dominique's mind. Just because she smacks her hand at 7:52 and says she's going to beat that ass doesn't necessarily mean she's going to kick Trina's ass. She might have been mad at 7:52 then forgot all about it by 8:52 and by 11:52 be smacking her hand declaring a beat-down on the lunch lady.

A whole lot can happen in one hour. How many hours are we in school? Eight? Nine? That's a lot of hours to be hot about nonsense. And isn't that the point? I don't know what any of it's about. I don't know if Dominique is playing or not, and why is that? It's none of my business.

Besides, I have my own crisis to deal with. My own priorities. So I take my own advice and raise my hand to get the pass from Mr. Adelman.

14

End of Song

LETICIA

IT'S NOT LIKE YOU'RE MISSING an actual class when you miss homeroom. I have nothing to gain by sitting through the rest of homeroom, especially when I have more pressing matters to deal with. Mr. Adelman agrees with me. He writes out my pass to the guidance counselor's office and I'm out the door.

"Look, Miss Olenbach. You have to put me back in Spanish."

She sings, "Leticia-a-a . . ."

I know all the words to the song. We've sung it so many times you'd think I'd be tired of her lyrics and mine.

"I told you. Spanish classes are overflowing. We have

more Spanish-speaking students this year. They need the classes. You know that."

"N-n-no I don't."

She sings, "Leticia-a-a . . . ," in two rising notes and one sinker.

I know my part and when to come in. I sing, "Miss Olenba-a-a-ach," low, high, high, low.

"Leticia, *what* can I do to make you understand?" Olenbach turns off the melody because I'm annoying her. I'm making her do her job—the one she should have done in the first place.

"This is what you can do. Put the Spanish-speaking kids in French. Even better, give them extra English classes. That should count for their foreign language. Just let me have Spanish. It's not too late to squeeze me into Señora Roberts's third-period class. I'll catch up."

"Oh, Leticia-a-a. Give French a chance." And we're back to the melody.

"Have you had French, Miss Olenbach? It's hard. At the end of class my jaw and my tongue be hurting. Feels like Madame LeCoeur reached in and twisted my tongue then socked me in the jaw. I hurt after that class. Really, Miss Olenbach. I hurt."

Miss Olenbach can't stop laughing. She thinks I'm the airhead teenage daughter in a sitcom. By closing my folder she clicks the power off on the remote, signifying *The Leticia Comedy Hour* is over. She remembers she's the adult here, excuses herself for laughing, and fixes her face.

"Haven't you ever felt good after doing something really difficult?" She has the nerve to ask me this, wearing a cashmere cardigan she didn't buy on a guidance counselor's paycheck.

"No," I tell her outright. "I avoid doing difficult things. Difficult doesn't do me any good. And *really* difficult?" I don't bother to finish. "Really difficult" isn't up for discussion.

"Come on, Leticia-a-a," she sings. "When you do something really hard, you feel accomplished. You take pride in your work. Your potential. Think of how good you'll feel when you pass this class after all your hard work. Don't you want to feel good about your work?"

"I honked like a goose in class today with Madame LeCoeur's hand on my throat. Would that make you feel good?"

She pushes out her chair, stands, and opens her arms. "You need a hug?"

I say, "No. I need a class change. All you have to do is turn on the computer, pull up Leticia Corinthia Moore, sophomore. Click 'no' on French I, click 'yes' on

Spanish III, third period, Señora Roberts."

She steps toward me, away from her desk, away from my file folder and the computer. I get the hint, get up, and say, "If my grade average goes down, it's your fault, Miss Olenbach."

She says, "Your average won't go down, Leticia. Not if you work."

"And if my schedule for next semester says zero-period French, I'm dropping out of school."

"Your parents won't let you drop out, Leticia." As if she knows Bridgette and Bernie Moore.

She places her hands on both my shoulders and steers me out of her office, singing, "Leticia-a-a. What am I going to do with you?"

It doesn't matter how many notes she sings, if they're high notes or sinkers. She wants me out of her office. End of song.

15

Turn It Around

DOMINIQUE

"HEY, TINY. Why ya cut out last night?"

"Yeah, Tiny. What's up?"

Only teammates call me Tiny. Not Shayne, not Viv, not Scotty. Reese slugs my shoulder. Bishop slaps my butt. Power center and star forward. Both seniors. Both stars. I'm good but they're trees skimming the rim. Six-one and six-two. Big, broad shoulders. One going to UConn, one going to Rutgers. Next stop, no stopping. They could go pro. I could turn on ESPN2 and be watching them battle. They're just like me. All-ball girls. See, I'm good. Real good. But without them there's no team. No wins. Without Reese and Bishop we're just girls in shorts running up and down the hardwood.

Even though I fight it, I'm smiling like a bitch in love. I tell them, "You all don't need me. You got Ellen."

They start slapping me around. Just playing like we do. Reese says, "Ellen's all right, but, Tiny, you're a guard."

That feels good, real good, but, I don't suck it all down. They're starting this Thursday and every game this season. I'm benched.

I say, "Tell Coach that. Tell Coach to put me back on the floor."

Yeah, see. One minute I'm a guard. Big love for Tiny. The next second there's silence. No one says a word.

"Come on, Reese. Bishop. You know I feed you. I take care of you on the court. The ball in my hands means the ball's in your hands. Come on."

Reese says, "You know Coach."

Bishop adds, "And Coach's rules."

You'll break before I bend the rules. Yeah. Heard it a thousand times. Coach's thing. Her saying.

Reese gives me a nice little shoulder slug. She says, "Just fix it, Tiny. You can do it. Turn it around."

I see him through the door's window. All alone in his hole. Little brown mouse. Hunched over in a curve, grading papers. Red pen up and little blue books in stacks.

I just want to talk. Just want Hershheiser to let me in. Hear me out. Understand that it's not just a science grade. It's not about lab work. I'm not trying to go to college when I get out. I'm not trying to be a doctor. A teacher. A lawyer. Colleges don't want shorties. Five-eight guards. They want trees. Trees to grow a championship on. They want Reese and Bishop to win big, and Ellen because she's Miss Who's Who. What does Coach call Ellen? An all-arounder: scholar-service-athlete. That's who colleges want. I get it. I'm not that.

I'm just a baller. A guard. A floor general running the show. Making plays happen on the court. That's from having eyes on the court; seeing where to be; beating the ball for the steal; reading the D; getting the ball in the hot hands, the open hands; charging into the paint or taking a charge; shooting from the high post.

All I have to do is make him understand that I need my minutes. My ball time while I can still get it. I'm not dumb. This is it. This and "the cage" on Fourth Street is what I got. I have to fight grown men just to be picked to play. They be knocking me down just to make me sit down. Ride the bench. Know my place. So this team is all the shot I get. I'm done once I'm out. So this can't come down to five points in science. This isn't "Do better next time, Dominique." This is "Fix it now."

I turn the knob but it won't move. It's locked. I'm on the outside and the little brown mouse is safe. I knock on the glass. *Rap/rap/rap.*

Little brown mouse looks up. He's way over by the window but I know those whiskers are twitching.

I use hand signs and say, *Mr. Hershheiser, let me talk to you.* I'm loud enough. He sees my hands motioning *Come here. Open up.* He hears me but he shakes his mouse head *No.*

"Come on, Hershheiser. I just want to talk. Make you understand."

He won't get out of his chair. He lifts his red pen and waves *No,* or *Shoo,* or *Go away,* or *I'm scared.*

Come on. Let me in. Let me talk. I just want to talk.

16

Like a Dead Saint

TRINA

NORMALLY I SIT THROUGH HOMEROOM and draw in my little notebook or chat with the guys to give them hope, but I can't sit myself still. I'm all shaky-shaky on the inside, my feet and my chair legs quake against the floor, Shakira-hip-shake fast. I can't sit still for another fifteen minutes. Not when I know Mr. Sebastian is hanging my artwork. None of my classes are near the gallery, so how would I get there to see the mural? I'll have to wait until lunch or until seventh and eighth period when I have Art. But I'm sorry. That is too long a time to wait. I just have to see my work and how Mr. Sebastian is hooking it up.

True, I admired my beauties when I had them spread out on the floor at home, but seeing them displayed in the gallery is entirely special. When you stand before all your work hanging up like that, you appreciate the colors, the music, the mixes. That's your work, your talent out on display. It's like the world can witness your greatness and you don't have to say a word.

I don't even have to lie. My homeroom teacher knows I have the antsies and lets me go.

Pobrecita. She needs a mirror. Doesn't she know how dumb she looks, waving her arms like an ape, banging against that teacher's door? Where is AP Shelton when kids are acting up?

Me, AP Shelton would catch, but boy-girl banging against the door—he'll walk the other way like she's invisible. What? Oh, who cares? Let me tiptoe down these stairs and skip over to the gallery.

Mwaam, mwaam, mwaam. Is it conceited to want to kiss your own work? I can truly, truly say I know what it is to be like Picasso. People will gather around and will not be able to move from wherever they're standing. This is even better than the "Oh, shnikies." Better and deeper. I could die right here and now, with my artwork the last thing I see, and I would die happy. Like I filled in that blank Ms. Bauer wanted me to complete in my journal.

Now, Mami wouldn't appreciate me leaving her all alone, but I would be like a dead saint and she would keep my room like a shrine and gaze at my artwork and miss me.

Oh, look. Mr. Sebastian gave me my own nameplate.

17

Damaged

LETICIA

I DON'T SEE THE PURPOSE OF GYM. You go down to the lockers. Three minutes. Take off your street shoes and take off your clothes. Three minutes. Remove your earrings, bracelets, chains, and rings. Two minutes. Put on your shorts and T-shirt, stretching the neck wide to protect your hair. Two minutes. Then put on your sneakers. Add it up. A lot of time already, right? Then you go to the gym, find your spot, and squat on that dirty floor a mop hasn't touched because there's only one janitor in this whole building. You watch Ms. Capito if you're in Part B, or Ms. Nunke if you're in Part A, demonstrate how to hit a ball, throw a ball, kick a ball, block a ball, catch a ball, and then for the next fifteen minutes it's your turn. You hit, throw, kick, block, or catch whatever ball it is. After, Ms. Capito blows the whistle and you run down to the lockers, throw yourself together in six minutes, and be in the hallway fresh and ready for the next period.

My point is, you spend more time changing than getting exercise, and if you care about your hygiene a little bit, you have to push some girl out the sink so you can splash water where you sweat, towel off, and roll on Secret. We have showers but my naked piggies aren't touching those mildewy tiles while that hard, rusty water hits my delicate skin. One janitor, remember?

Gym is one inconvenience on top of another. It might be a big-girl thing but I don't like to sweat. Nothing good comes from hard work and sweat dripping off your body. For one, you stink, and you don't want stink-dried stains under your arms when you sit next to Chem II James in eighth period. All because you put effort into catching, kicking, and running after a ball. Leave that to Dominique and the gym leaders. Leave that to folks who care. All I have to do to pass this class is get dressed, line up, bounce whatever ball we're bouncing once, then get back into my clothes. That will get me a 70 and enough credits to move on to the next round.

Today we're all lined up, six girls by six girls, doing arm raises. I'm hiding behind Anabel Winkler because Anabel stands out with her long arms and legs. If Ms. Capito focuses on Anabel, she's not focusing on me. My arms are sort of up. Not over my head, but you shouldn't be able to see that. I'm chilling, not sweating.

Just when I think she's not paying me any mind, Capito snags me anyway. "Come on, Moore. This is good for you." She strolls between the rows with her whistle and clipboard. Ms. Capito is cute with her Dutch boy haircut, those tight little muscles on her pencil legs and arms. But don't let that little lady fool you. Ms. Capito doesn't mess around. Ms. Capito demands all-out participation, which is why I hide behind Anabel.

"I'm doing it," I say. "See?" This time I raise my arms a smidge higher, making a wide V. All the way up and all the way down makes you sweat. This is only one of the warm-up exercises. I'm pacing myself.

"All the way. Come on, Moore. You can do it."

"How's this good for me, Ms. Capito? You know I'm sensitive to sweat."

"You're fat. This will break up that lard."

Ms. Capito will snap on you without smiling. Lucky for her this isn't a new conversation. No one laughs or waits for my reaction. Instead her snap sounds weak, like she's saying "How ya doing, Leticia?" I don't stress. I know she loves me.

"Sweating is good, Moore. If you'd shake it up, you'd sweat. You sweat, you lose."

"What makes you think I want to lose anything? I want all this here."

Plus I have asthma. I do. I'm supposed to take my time and not exert myself. I'm supposed to take it easy.

Ours is one of the biggest gyms in the city. The wooden divider keeps two boys' classes on one side while we have two girls' classes going on this side—Gym Part A and Gym Part B. We're both learning volleyball, except our class is a day behind Nunke's class. I know that because they already did what we're doing today. We're learning how to pass it to each other. They're smacking it hard over the net. It's not that I care what's going on in Part A, but it dawns on me when I look over there. Dominique is in Part A with Ms. Nunke.

I don't want to stare at Dominique too hard but I can't turn away either. She wants Nunke to let her smack the ball but Ms. Nunke sends Dominique to the end of the line. It's kind of funny, but I don't want Basketball Jones catching me grinning. You know she used to carry her basketball—I'm not lying—to class, until AP Shelton made her stop.

I face front. Who knows what sets her off. I mean, what did Trina do to her, besides skip by being Trina?

And even if I saw what I thought I saw, maybe it's over. A thing of the moment. Over and forgotten. Now all she wants is her turn at the net. She's not thinking about Trina.

I don't know why Bea's getting all excited. All *You gotta tell her, Leticia.*

Capito says, while our gym leader demonstrates, "Raise your hands with your elbows bent, forming a triangle. Cup your hands slightly, like this. Then release!"

I look at the gym leader and do what she does. Hold my hands, fingers curved, then pop my fingers open for the release. We do that ten times in a row. Triangle, cup, pop. I'm not sweating so I don't mind the finger exercises. I admire the shooting stars on my square-tipped nails while I cup and release my fingers.

The gym leader pops and releases the ball up into the air. Capito runs under the ball, holds her hands up in the triangle, and then pops it back. The ball balloon floats between them. They stand in place, not even running for the ball. Not grunting or sweating. Just lightly popping the ball back and forth. I almost like it. It looks easy.

"Imagine the sun setting," Capito says, "and it's hot. You don't want to get burned so you release it quickly with your fingertips." Then she pairs us with partners so we can pass the white floaty sun back and forth.

I say to Anabel, "Look. I'm not running to get under the ball, so set it right."

Tall Anabel says, "I'm just gonna throw. Whatever happens, happens."

I make the triangle and wait.

Anabel doesn't even try to set the sun like Capito showed us. Instead she throws the ball over my head and I look at her, then I look at the ball sail by.

"I'm not chasing after no ball."

Anabel stands there tapping her large sneaker. She's not chasing after it either.

Another girl kicks the ball to me and I kick the ball back to Anabel. This time when Anabel tosses it up, it falls just right. I don't even have to move. Just cup my fingers into the triangle and tell myself, *Here comes the sun. Don't get burnt.* And I pop my fingers to release the ball, like Capito showed us. Then—

Pop!

My nail! My silk-wrapped, hand-painted, custom-designed, three-quarter-inch, square-cut nail tip with the sparkling faux diamond flies off my finger and shoots across the gym. I am knocking down girls in white Ts and blue shorts to rescue my custom-designed nail. As I

91

rush to my nail, all of those months of manicure appointments, fillings, and retouches flash before me. I dive and scoop up my nail tip, saving it from being crushed by some girl thoughtlessly running to get under a volleyball.

I am so busy blowing gym dirt off my custom-designed nail and assessing the damage that I am just now feeling the pain inflicted by that volleyball. And then I see my hand. My damaged hand. Four perfectly painted silk-wrapped nails and one fat and useless finger standing out, dead center.

I march up to Capito and shove my custom-designed, hand-painted nail tip at her.

"Who's gonna pay for this?"

She says, "Pay for what?"

"My silk-wrapped tip, Ms. Capito. Who gonna pay?"

She laughs at me like we was doing our daily joke, but joke time is over. I am serious.

"Someone's got to pay," I tell her. "Someone's got to take responsibility. This cost money. This happened here and you're the adult in charge. What are you going to do about this, Ms. Capito?"

Ms. Capito holds my hand to get a good look, then says, "I'll write you a pass to get it cleaned up."

I snatch my hand back. "I don't care about a pass. I want action. I've been damaged."

18
All-Ball Girl

DOMINIQUE

I LIKE GYM. I don't cut gym. I don't have a problem with gym. Just folk dancing. I'll sit out if we're folk dancing. Big cramps if we're do-si-do'ing.

Just give me ball days. Show off my ball skills. My hustle. My drive. I'm here for ball days. I'll suit up. I'll play. Yeah. Give me all ball days. I'm an all-ball girl.

Brown ball. That's my thing. That's me. Spanking the court with the brown ball, passing, shooting. Brown ball is fitted for my hands. The right fit in the curve of my hand. Only feels wrong when the ball's not sucked into the curve of my hand. Vacuum sucked. If it's up to me, we'll play brown ball all year long. All-ball girl.

But I'll play what we got. Any ball. Toss it here. I'll play it. Throw it. Hit it. Defend it. Score it. Knock it down. Just let it be a ball day. Not a health film day. Not a folk-dancing day. As long as it's a ball day, I'll play. You know it: all-ball girl.

We're still on the white ball. Volleyball. Nunke and the gym leader, Crawford, demonstrate the spike at the net. Nunke throws the ball up. The ball arcs right. Crawford, in that white student leader uniform, runs and leaps like she's in ballet class. Runs, leaps like she's in a tutu. Runs, leaps, and taps the white ball with her open hand. Just a tap. A ballerina tap. And they do it again. Up, arc, then run, leap, tap.

Enough demonstrations. We get it. Let's do it.

We line up for our turn at the net. Our turn to do it. Spike it over the net. I jump to the front, but Nunke points to the back. "Come on," I say. Nunke says, "Back of the line, Duncan," sounding like Coach. I can't believe she won't let me slide, but she's not hearing me. She points. "Back, Duncan." So I go back. The last girl on line.

It's all right. I'll get my shot. That's what I tell myself while I wait. I watch Nunke set it and the girls try to hit it. Nunke sets it up, right. And if a girl misses it, she doesn't go to the end of the line. That's your turn, you're done. Scram. No. Crawford throws the ball back to Nunke and Nunke sets it again.

And I'm watching the clock. Watching the misses. Counting the girls on line. Thirty, forty girls ahead of me. A minute a girl. And all I want is a hit. Just one, just one. Let me hit one.

I'm tasting it. When my turn comes up, it won't be about run. It won't be about leap. It won't be about tap. When Nunke sets it straight up, as it falls a little to the right, I'll charge the net, haul back, and *kablam*. A hammer slam. My hand's throbbing, from the back of the line. Throbbing. I'm tasting the smack of the ball. The white, soft, hard leather. That feels good against your hand, yo. That sting is so good, your skin turns white, and then the blood comes back. It hurts, but that hard, hard slap is good. And you want that soft white ball one more time. One more hit.

Let me get one. Let me get one. One good hit. One solid slap.

The line is moving. I'm two girls away. But I take my eye off the clock for a second and the bell rings. Once that bell rings it's chickens fleeing the coop. All balls drop. All the little chick-chicks go running to the lockers, but I grab Crawford and say, "Hey. Just one. Set me up one."

She says, "I gotta go."

I pick up the white ball and throw it at her. Crawford's

quick. She's not a gym leader for nothing. She catches it and gives in.

"Just one," she says.

"That's all I asked for." So I'm in position, right. A few feet from the net, strong side. I'm looking up, ready to charge, haul back, and slap that ball down. She sets, but she doesn't set it right. I can get a piece of it, but it's too low. I'd have to tap it and I'm not here to tap nothing.

"No, no. That's not it. Put it up. Straight up."

Crawford knows she ain't going nowhere until she does it right. So she sets it, perfect frog arms spring, and it's up, straight up, ninety degrees. I'm off. I'm charging. I'm under it, and it's hanging in the sweet spot, and *pss-slap!* Hammer to the nail. A spinning rocket to the back court line. That was good contact. Good slap. Good sting. My hand is burning. I could hit another.

19

Slamming on the Brakes

LETICIA

I CAN'T MISS AP SHELTON standing in the stream of kids, and he can't miss me, headed right at him. Our eyes lock. There's no turning away from me.

"Miss Moore," he says.

"AP Shelton," I say right back. "I was damaged in your school and I want to know what you intend to do about it."

AP Shelton is the right person for this job. He is a serious man. He scrunches the lines in his forehead, taking in the gravity of my complaint. He's ready to do what assistant principals do.

"Walk with me to my office," he says. His voice dips low, in a hush. "I want to know exactly what happened."

We're walking but I can't contain myself. Something must be done now. The sooner he knows, the sooner he

97

can take action. I thrust my disfigured hand in his face. I want him to see what class participation got me. I say, "I hope this school has insurance, because this happened in your gymnasium during a volleyball exercise."

AP Shelton slams on the brakes. We're no longer speeding to his office. He looks at my wounded hand and my severed silk-wrapped nail tip and says, "Go to class, Miss Moore."

I can't breathe. Not even Bridgette and Bernie believe me when I say I have asthma, but I feel an attack coming on. I manage to find a breath and say, "But my hand. My hand is damaged."

He sighs. *Sighs.* That only makes my outrage climb. In fact, my outrage is halfway to heaven.

"Go to the girls' bathroom and run cold water over it. I'll write you a pass."

I stamp my feet. "I don't want a pass. I want action. I was damaged during gym. My hand and my property. Someone has to pay. Someone has to be responsible."

He alternately nods yes and no and sings, "Oh, I agree, Miss Moore."

Is that a smirk? A smirk and a song? Oh no, he didn't just smirk at me in my hour of pain and loss of property. I tell him, "My parents will be in your office bright and early, AP Shelton. They'll want to talk to you."

Now it's out-and-out smirking. He says, "Good, Miss Moore. I'll want to talk to them."

"I'm serious, AP Shelton."

"Go to class, Miss Moore."

I need to make a call. I can't worry about getting caught with Celina because this is a medical emergency. Instead of going to class I slip inside the Media Center. Mrs. Thomas, the media specialist, is tucked away in her little office, so I duck down into a PC cubicle, stay low, and hit 1 on speed dial for Bridgette.

"What's the matter?"

"Mommy, it's bad. It's so bad."

"What, 'Ticia? Tell me."

"We have to sue the school, Mommy."

"*What?*"

Her heels are clicking, like she's walking away so she can explode in private. That's right, Bridgette. Let that outrage climb sky-high.

"For what they made me do."

It was quiet on the other end. She's having palpitations, imagining the worst, which is how it should be.

"They made me participate in volleyball."

"What?"

"Volleyball, Mommy," I said. "They made me set the sun and hit the sun and the ball hit me and tore off my custom-designed nail tip. The one with the faux diamond."

" 'Ticia. Is this why you called me at my job? Do you know I'm in the middle of a presentation? Do you know I have an office full of people waiting on me and you're telling me about some volleyball and some fake nail? Girl . . ."

"It broke down to the skin, Mommy. The meat and everything. I can't even write. My hand is in pain."

"Go to the nurse's office. Put some ice on it."

"But I can't write or hold nothing in this hand."

"You holding the phone, aren't you?"

"Mommy."

"Deal. It's only temporary, 'Ticia."

"Didn't you hear me? My nail didn't just chip. It broke. I can barely move my finger, it's so swollen. And the school's not doing anything about it."

She is puffing hot air on the other end. Celina picks up all of that. "What do you want from me?"

Is that any way to talk to your only child? The only child you will ever have? Is that how you do your beloved child?

"Mommy, please come to school to pick up my nail and then go to the Golden Blossom Nail Salon and give Girl Number Four twenty dollars to fix it. Tell her I have it wrapped in tissue so she doesn't have to create a new one."

There is a long silence, like our connection has been dropped. Celina does the best she can but sometimes Celina drops the ball.

Finally she says, " 'Ticia, honey. It can wait for Friday. Saturday."

"Mommy, didn't you hear me? It's a deep wound. Down to the flesh. I can't do anything with this hand. It can't wait for Friday or Saturday."

Then there is nothing. Dead nothing. In fact, the screen goes from CALL to wallpaper. I hit redial. I aim Celina just right so she has three bars. My little girl is trying to get that connection. Celina's ringing, ringing. Pick up, Bridgette. It's your baby. Pick up.

I gasp. It's worse than AP Shelton slamming on the brakes outside his office. Bridgette either turned her phone off or swiped IGNORE CALLER.

It takes me a minute to recover. Outrage on top of outrage. I only have so much time, so I pull myself together and hit 2 on speed dial.

"Daddy . . ."

By the time I finish it's understood that Bernie is to skip lunch, pick up the nail at school, and then drive down to the Golden Blossom Nail Salon and pay Girl Number Four—the one with the mole on her left earlobe—twenty dollars for Big Sweetie. That's what Girl Number Four calls me. Big Sweetie. "And leave her a tip, Daddy. A good tip so she'll take care of me."

I know how to look out for people, and I don't appreciate a sloppy job.

20
You're Going Down

"CARMEN, YOU SAW IT, up on C Corridor? What did you—"

*"Down
You're going down
Unh/unh stomp-stomp-stomp
Unh/unh stomp-stomp-stomp
You're going down."*

Aw, yeah! They're doing my stomp. Cup of spinach and slice of pizza has to wait. I got to get in on this.

"Watch my tray, Carmen?"

*"Slap butt, stomp-stomp-stomp
Slap that booty, stomp-stomp-stomp
You're going down."*

In I jump, next to Mikki on the end. Right in time to come in on

"*down*
Unh/unh stomp-stomp-stomp
Unh/unh stomp-stomp-stomp
You're going down."

How fly does that look? Me and the Boosters stomping feet, shaking booty, doing the cheer, five right hands pointing in unison:
"down
You're going down
Slap/slap/slap
Going down."

Oh! Here's my part. In double time:
"*Slap/slap/slap/slap/slap/slap*
Unh/unh/unh/unh/unh/unh
Clap/clap/clap/clap/clap/clap
Stomp/stomp/stomp/stomp/stomp/stomp
down."

Mikki's going off, yo. Her feet are so fast it's like she's trying to lose me, but I keep up. I don't disappoint my girl. For her "Unh/unh/unh" I've got "Unh/unh/unh/unh/unh/unh." And I'm laughing, not huffing and puffing. Stomping tight with the Boosters. They're in their blue tees. And I'm the hot-pink dot. The standout in the exclamation point. What? The lunch crowd is wowed by the hot pink. The hot chick. All you hear is

Mikki, Renee, Connie, Pam, and Trina. Go, Trina. Go, Trina.

Jonesy, Malik, Devin, and the rest of the basketball team all want me to try out for cheerleaders. I'm like their lucky charm. They want me on the floor in the crunch. Can you see me out there, in the short-short skirt, the tight blue V-neck, and white pom-poms? Angie, the head cheerleader, gets blue and white stars painted on her cheeks for games. Don't get me started painting colors on my face. All my fabulous mixes. What?

I was gassed when they begged me. "For you, Malik, I'll try out." But first I went to check out the squad, and thank God I saw it for myself. All I can say is no cheerleading for Trina. Angie, Nettie, and them only have two cute cheers. The rest of it is posing, doing air traffic controller signing, keeping their arms stiff and their hands fisted. They make a pyramid and who do you suppose climbs to the tip-top of nine girls? Body untouchable tight, little, and perfect, that's who. You can't throw me in the back. People would say, Where's the cute one? Don't get me wrong. Angie, Nettie, and the other girls on the squad look good. You can't have ugly cheerleaders. Your girls take the floor and the other team points and laughs at your ugly cheerleaders. Forget about cheering the game. The other squad got cheers for the ugly girls' faces alone.

Pretty cheerleaders aren't stereotypes. Pretty cheerleaders with bouncy hair and pom-poms are a necessity.

But see, I'm already pretty. I need to bounce. I need to shake it with a bang. Stomp in double time. Not pose and crash from the top of the pyramid. I'm practically in with the Boosters. And they wear those cute tight sweats with the matching hoodie. Add the stomp/stomp/stomp with the famous Trina shaky-shake and you set off a frenzy. The cafeteria is on fire.

So I'm going back to my table to have my pizza, collect my rah-rahs, listen to everyone tell me about my art in the gallery and my stomping with the Boosters. I thought Mikki, Pam, Renee, and Connie were about to sit down but they're starting up another cheer.

"Carmen, please, please. Just watch it for me." We're getting ready to go again. They'll want me with them. Pizza's getting cold but I'll eat it hard and cold later.

"When they get it we say, 'Miss it!'
M-I-S-S I-T MISS IT!
M-I-S-S I-T MISS IT!
When we steal it we say, 'Sink it!'
S-I-N-K I-T SINK IT!
S-I-N-K I-T SINK IT!
And the feet go—"
Aw yeah. The whole lunchroom is stomping.

Uh-oh. The lunch cops get up and stroll to the center of the cafeteria to cool things down. I call out to Officer DaCosta, "Hey."

She keeps a straight, tight face.

"I bet you didn't know I had so much talent."

She remembers me from the early morning. From the smile I put on her face.

"It's lunchtime, not dance time," Officer DaCosta says.

Officer DaCosta's got juice. The cafeteria starts to chill.

Mikki, Renee, Connie, and Pam go to their table. I know I should join them but I can't leave Carmen sitting there with my cold pizza and spinach. That wouldn't be right.

21

Break Me Off a Piece

DOMINIQUE

I'M TRYING TO EAT THIS MEATBALL SUB. Trying to chew, get it down. But it's noisy and crazy in here and the Boosters are stomping, french fries flying—better not fly this way—and Scotty gotta push up on me from behind, wrap himself around me, and I'm not in the mood. I don't even want the sub.

Scotty's like a kid tied to his mother's lap. If she gets up to pee he's holding on.

I push him off me, but he's—*zzt*—clamped on like a magnet. I push, he clamps on. Push harder, clamp-clamp. Scotty's like a kid and like a dog. "Sit, Scott. Sit while I shoot hoops." "Fetch, Scott. Fetch me a water." Sit, fetch, stay. But Scotty's loyal. Puppy loyal with those big eyes. Does what I tell him. *Awright. Stay, Scott. You can stay.*

Shayne starts singing the candy bar song. "Break me

off a piece of that KitKat bar." She knows I'm about to give her a tap. A little punch. So she leans back in time.

Once I broke Scotty off a piece I was stuck with him. Broke him off a piece and now he wants another. He needs to get over that. It was a one-time shot. A thing of the moment.

I was mad and had to do something and mad sex is some good shit, yo. It's some good, mad shit. I never did that before. Not all the way. But Coach benched me and steam was rising out of my skin. Yo, I was suited up, game ready. Dressed. Ready to play. And Coach was like, "Duncan. Bench," like I'm some dog. *Stay on that bench. That's where you're going to be for the rest of the season.* "Duncan. Bench." And I was mad like, what's that movie? Yeah. Mad like *Raging Bull.* So now I know why they call it "hitting it." 'Cause I was that mad and I needed to hit something or have something hit me so I made Shayne and Viv walk up. *Y'all just keep walking and we'll catch up.* It was dark. After five. So I pulled Scotty over to the side of the building, right. The Hunan Palace. And I pulled out his thing and said, "Hit it." And those big eyes . . . was like all, but I wasn't in the mood for all that. I was like, "Hit it." Scotty had my back banging against the brick wall. Against the brick wall of the Hunan Palace. Mad heat was pouring down my legs and all I could hear was "Duncan. Bench." "Duncan. Bench." "Duncan. Bench."

Scotty reaches for a fry. I don't care. They're cold. Hard. No wonder kids throw them like weapons.

Viv says, "Someone needs to make her sit down."

I tell them, "Don't worry. I got that. I'm'o sit her pink ass down."

Me and Viv and Shayne are laughing and watching the bitch, watching the bitch. Yea, pink bitch. Stink bitch. That's right. Get your stomp on. Get your shake on. 'Cause you will get stomped. You will get shaken. I tell my girls, "It's on."

We're laughing and Scotty's eyes get bigger. He wants to know what's going on. Why we're looking over there. At the Boosters and that pink chick.

It's as loud as hell in here. Crazy. The Boosters are singing that cheer. That "You going down" cheer. Viv starts singing along with them: "You're going down— with a big crush." And Shayne pipes in "At two forty-five, go-ing down." And it's all to the beat.

22

It's On

LETICIA

IT'S HARD TO EAT LEFT-HANDED but I don't want anybody staring at my right hand. Two tables over, Dominique's guy is hugging her up, but I'm not thinking about what's going on with Dominique. Chem II James is walking down with his tray, searching for a spot to sit, and I'm praying he doesn't park his tray at my table. I'm praying today isn't the day he finds me irresistible and must be in my presence. I'll forget myself, break out into my "cute and can't be bothered" mode, flash my hands, thinking they're both still gorgeous, and then he'll see my deformed hand.

It's so loud in here between the usual roar and the Boosters practicing that I can't hear myself pray, and . . . can you believe this? Trina is stomping with the Boosters.

Chem II James takes a seat near the Boosters. And

Trina. He doesn't look this way because he's looking that way. So I toss my head, as if anyone notices, only to find myself facing Dominique's table. I'm looking dead at Dominique, Vivica, and Shayne, reading their lips like a deaf-mute pro. Vivica and Shayne are singing to the beat of the Boosters' cheer, but Dominique is straight up saying it: *You're going down.*

I try to pull away to not make it obvious that I'm staring at them but my eyes are locked onto their table. It's like a movie that's about to heat up and the dun/

dun/

dun

music plays because stuff is about to go down and you don't dare blink or get up to go to the bathroom.

Just look at Trina. It would be almost funny if you didn't already know she was about to get beat down. And it's on. As sure as I'm holding a slice of pizza with my left hand, it is on. Trina's just jumping, shaking, and stomping. Showing off that "hot chick" plastered on the seat of her pink KMarts without a clue.

Now that it's definitely on, and I know I saw what I saw, I can honestly say I have no sympathy and this is all Trina's fault. If Bea were here in the caf instead of working in the "real world" she'd have no sympathy either. No matter how you look at it, Trina don't have anyone to blame but Trina. I don't know what she did to Basketball Jones but she put herself in this fix. Just look at her. She's doing it right now. Sticking herself somewhere uninvited. Look at Mikki and them. They'd jump her now if there wasn't a cop stationed in every corner. They don't want her stepping with them. They didn't invite her, but there is Trina, soaking up their moment. Being where she shouldn't be. Dominique might be wrong, and it might be trifling, but this is all Trina's fault.

When you're the outsider, you should know your situation. Know who you are when you step out. Know what you can do and can't do. Know whose face you can be in and whose joke you can laugh at. You should know whose man belongs to who, and even if he's on his own, you should know where he was before you came skipping along. You can't just arrive on the scene and be jumping in everyone's face. You gotta know where to step and how.

Even worse, not only is Trina flunking rules and history, she doesn't have any people. If everyone knows your brothers, sisters, cousins, and the people you're cool with, you have protection. An invisible ring of your people and their people around you. Don't mess with Bea, 'cause she's with Jay. Don't mess with Jay 'cause he can handle himself and he got people. Don't mess with Leticia because she's with Bea. And then Bea with Jay, and there's the invisible ring, and so on. So if you have beef with Leticia, you have to say, Do I want to have beef with Jay and his crew? See how this works? Trina don't have people. She thinks she do, but she don't have anyone but Trina and that pink outfit she got on.

Poor Mikki, Renee, and them. Trying to shake Trina, but she's the chunky peanut butter clinging to the bread.

Just in time. The lady cop and her squad are on the job, shutting down the Boosters. But look at Trina. She can't just walk back to her table. She got to do that shaky-shake thing like she can't get enough attention. And that's why Trina can't blame anyone but Trina for this mess. So no. I don't have to tell Trina a thing. This might even be good for her. She might learn a lesson.

23
Boy-girls

TRINA

THE NOISE IN THE CAF melts to a low roar. The pizza is hard and rubbery, but drinking the milk and feeling the love all around me makes the chewy dough go down smooth. And there's much love everywhere I turn. Trina art-up-on-C-Corridor love. Trina stomping-with-the-Boosters love. Much love for Trina wearing hot pink. Love all around.

When you got it, you want to spread it. Even over there, across the bench where Griffy and Pheoma slouch. Those girls need to feel the love. Always with the anger, those two. The hate. The punching. Don't even look at them like they're not girls because they swear they are. What? *Oh yeah, we're girls.* But they don't even try. They don't have enough natural goodness to stretch, roll, and go in the morning. They need color. Lotion.

Effort. Girls like Griffy and Pheoma, boy-girls, are not straight-out lezzies. Not like Dara and India and Nadira and them. Pheoma and Griffy aren't hand-holding, smooching-in-B-Corridor, dressing-each-other-up-for-the-prom lezzies. No. Pheoma, like Griffy—who knows her real name?—are stone boy-girls. Big, beefy boy-girls with small knotted ponytails. Not bouncy-shiny-silky tails like mines. Theirs is like, *Yo, let's handle this hair, wrestle it down with a rubber band so it don't get in the way when we're smacking that handball into the wall.* But they're girls. You can't tell them otherwise. They're just boy-girls and they get mad if you look at them like, *Know your role, boy-girl.*

Have you ever heard the whack of a ball against a hand then against the wall? Not with these gorgeous hands. Hitting a hard rubber ball against the wall. Your palm turns to shoe leather from smacking it around. Nasty orange calluses crust up where it should be soft to tease a boy's neck.

Once, I saw Pheoma and Griffy kick these freshmen, a couple of boys, off the handball court. That was sad funny, yo. You couldn't help but laugh. These girls just rode up on those poor guys, took the ball while it was in play, bounced it off the concrete wall, and then threw it over the fence into the street. Griffy took out her rubber ball and she and Pheoma started smacking it up against the wall.

The two boys, those freshmen, were like, *Hey!* And the boy-girls were like, *What?* and it was over. Almost. One boy wanted to be like, *What?* back and tried to step, arms in motion, like he could do something. I prayed to God right there for his life. It was about to get ugly on the handball court for those little boys. Against those boy-girls. *What?* But God intervened through the other boy and grabbed him while his arm was waving. He said, "Let those dykes have it." And even though his face wasn't showing it, you know he was glad his friend stepped in, so they laughed and called Pheoma and Griffy dykes while they were walking away. Big steps, like running away.

And Basketball Girl. Dominique? Yeah. Dominique. She don't hang with Griffy and Pheoma but she's a stone boy-girl. Big NBA-shirt-wearing boy-girl with a cute guy hanging on her, tagging behind her. *What?* Cannot lie. Scotty is too hot for Dominique. Hot and pretty. Scotty could be the dream prom date in a teen magazine. With those eyes and that curly hair and model lips. Pouty. So pouty I want to smear lip gloss on him. Tangerine mixed with berry on those *mwaam, mwaam, mwaam* lips. Can you imagine lips like those saying "Baby"—I'm not even on to the kiss.

Damn! What did Basketball Girl do to deserve that? Scotty must like that manly stuff because Dominique is built like a rig. The kind that hauls a fleet of brand-new cars. And he likes that. Go figure. But yeah, Dominique's a stone boy-girl. Ponytail, jeans, big-ass lumberjack shirt like she Brawny Girl. Never wears pinks, violets, or orange—*naranja* would go perfect with her skin! Never shows off her curves. You only see her legs on the court. I know she got scars. I was passing by Fourth Street Park in my cute T with the V and my shorts, blending in with the flowers, the greenery, beautifying the neighborhood. And who do you see pushing up the court like an ape, low to the asphalt, ball in one hand, other hand curled, *oo-hoo-oo-hoo*. Then she charges them, right? And a guy knocks her down and she gets up and I can see the blood on her knees, and I'm sorry, but what is a girl doing aping around with those gorillas? They aren't even boys. They're men with man stink pouring out to the sidewalk. And Scotty sitting on the park bench watching his sweetie getting knocked down by those men. But she got all those scars on her legs. Scotty don't see those scars or he likes all that. Maybe she don't wear a skirt to spare us from seeing those scabby legs. That can't be pretty. But she got Scotty.

I couldn't have a boyfriend that pretty. I mean,

Scotty's *too* pretty. Where would people focus when they see us together? That's why they hang masterpieces apart, so people can appreciate each one. But hey. Dominique never looks concerned and Scotty's sticking with his ape girl. His boy-girl. His eighteen-wheeler rig.

He is still too pretty.

Silent *mwack* to Scotty.

24

Girl Fights

LETICIA

YOU CAN FEEL IT UP and down A, B, and C. Girl fight. Girl fight. No one's talking about it but the buzz is there, like the gray wall tiles are there. It's in everyone's eyes. Eager, like how you feel standing outside a party where they're playing the hot dance jam and you can't wait to get inside. Rocking hot excitement. Lotta bright eyes, lotta yeahs and unh-hms. Thick. Everywhere.

No one cares about guys fighting. That's like, so what. You see that in the halls during bell change. But girl fights are something else. Girls don't show off their skills when they fight. They don't hold up their dukes and weave their heads side to side like cobras and come out quickstepping. Unlike two guys getting down, girls don't try to look pretty. You know what boxing is, right? Two guys dancing and ducking to see who can stay pretty longest.

Don't let me be in my room on Friday night during fight time. Don't let it be a pay-per-view match. Bernie confuses me with the son he never had and must share the boxing experience with his baby. *'Ticia, pretty, come watch this fight with your daddy.*

Like I did when I could still sit on his lap. We're a long way from lap days but I'm still Daddy's baby girl. Sports don't thrill me one way or the other, but I need new clothes. My closet is stuffed with last year's rags and I like those skirts that came out this year—but the genuine article—not those Canal Street knockoffs. You think I'd be caught wearing fake shit? I'm a Big Girl. I can't wear nobody's fake shit. You know those factory workers packed in a basement are too hungry and delirious to concentrate on the stitching. The fabric and thread are cheap too. Can you imagine, I'm walking down B Corridor and *rrrip*! Talk about mad and embarrassed. My stuff out in the open. So no. I can't collect my weekly pennies from Bridgette and Bernie, hop the downtown train to Canal Street to push through the Chinese and whatnot to save a dollar on weak denim that'll split and show my Vicky Secrets to the world. You know Vickys don't cover it. Like I said, I'm a Big Girl. I gotta have my rags stitched right.

Anyway, I give in, sink into the leather next to Bernie, lean in like I care, but it's all the same Friday night fight to me. Bernie's happy. He has his baby girl, the hi-def hookup, hot wings, and some beer. What more could he want on fight night?

Two guys in silk shorts and matching sneaker boots touch gloves at the center of the ring. They have pretty names like Sugar This, Pretty Boy That, not Don't Mess With Me, cause-I-will-take-these-ten-ounce-gloves-and-thump-your-head-deep-in-your-neck names. They spring back, dancing, showing each other their steps. The first two rounds their silk shorts bounce, sneakers shuffle, heads weave to connect and miss light taps to the air and almost to the rib cage, which the announcer calls the Sweet Science. By round three the gloves are heavy so out come the jabs. They pad a one-two-three to the body, then *wooohm-wooohm* to the face, the eyes especially, to score that blood. The bell clangs, and Sugar dances to his corner, Pretty Boy to his, and I'm not even thinking about that hoochie in heels and bikini holding up the ROUND 4 card. The cut man takes a razor to Sugar's puffed-shut lids so Sugar can see, while on the other side the corner man reaches into Pretty's mouth and yanks out that nasty mouthpiece so Pretty can spit blood into a bucket. Now remember: hi-def hookup in the living room. Blood, teeth, sweat coming through the screen. I have to wipe my cheek. Why anyone pays money to see this, I can't tell you, but don't no one ask me if I work hard for my extra allowance. I fake pick a boxer to win and fake cheer for his red satin shorts. And if there's a main event, I stick around for that too. I earn my extra change—plus I throw in some love for Bernie. And if Daddy peels me off a bill or two—Daddy's not stupid, he knows I'm on the clock—then I worked hard. That's right. I earned those bills. I can go to Bloomie's or Macy's and try stuff on, and send the girl out on the floor to fetch me another skirt in my size. That's right. Let her work for a change.

You can say that it's not work watching a couple of guys in silk shorts dancing around showing off their skills, but I put in the time. I do the work. And the two guys are about showing off their skills.

Girl fights? Girl fights aren't hardly about showing off skills. Girl fights are ugly. Girl fights are personal.

25
Hey

TRINA

"HEY."

"Hey."

"Tree-na."

"Hey."

Feel all this love. Popular. What? So many fans. So many friends and so many who want to be. They either caught the shaky-shake and stomp in the caf or they saw my artwork in the gallery. I need a Princess Di wave. No diamond tiara because I have my lucky gold chain and all my subjects adore me. The love keeps pouring.

"Trina. He-ey."

"Hey."

Back in my old school, I spent more time at home on the sofa watching soaps, TV judges, and paternity shows than I spent in class. What can I say? The old school was full of haters. You know how it is—fresh out of middle school, you're still a little wild. Still surprised by everything going on with you. So you look at someone who is cool with everything and you're hating because you're like, "What does she know that I don't?" Translation: I wish I could be her.

And my appendix burst in gym. That also kept me home on the sofa. They should have believed me when I said I had pain. No one believed me until I was down on the wooden floor sweating, clutching my side. Then they believed. The ambulance came in a flash.

But it was cool. It all worked out for the best. I don't mind repeating because I know I'm not dumb. I'm not lazy. I just spent too many days home. It didn't matter how much my teachers loved me or how well I did, it all came down to the number of days. "We love you, Trina, but you've had too many days out. What can we do?"

The guidance counselor truly loved me. "Trina," she said, "you're gifted."

Yes, yes. I know.

"You have a talent for beauty. Color."

You can't miss that.

"I've been talking to your teachers and we agree that you have an aptitude for art."

No one had used a word like that for me. *Aptitude.*

She didn't have to explain it. I got it. I have the *habilidad*. I am apt to make beauty and color.

"Look at this brochure. This is your new school." Her last few words played like music. She said, "They have an art program."

The brochure was made of heavy, high-gloss paper. When the guidance counselor put it down before me, the crease made a loud *croc* against the desk. It was serious paper. Of course they show the school building and kids smiling on the cover, and now that you go here you know that those kids must have been cutting. And then you open the brochure and like the heavy, slick feeling of the paper. It isn't throwaway paper. Inside they have all the high school things: the basketball team, the student government, the science lab, and tucked in the corner, the art program. A man with too much hair and a mustache is showing a girl how to draw. I didn't know at the time it was Mr. Sebastian, but I put my face where the girl's face was. Next year some girl would see my face in the new brochure on serious high-gloss paper and wish she were me.

I knew this was the right place from the beginning. Everyone was like, "Hey," when they saw me coming down B Corridor. And the school has this art program where Mr. Sebastian calls the classrooms studios. C Corridor outside our studio is the gallery. When we're painting or sketching or sculpting we're artists. When he needs to get us quiet we are "Class," in that flat duck-quack voice. We like being artists. It's a different feeling from being a Math or Biology or Social Studies student. Mr. Sebastian plays music while we work. A lot of strings and horns and piano fighting for air, but we're used to it. He gives us a different language in that class and he expects us to use it. Like, you can't say "That's deep." You have to say "That has texture" and "Those colors are vibrant." You have to use the artist language. "When you're in Spanish class, you speak Spanish, yes?" he says. "Well, we speak art in the studio."

It was hard, speaking art, in the beginning. The first few weeks when we were getting to know each other Mr. Sebastian stayed on my case for using "pretty" and "cute" and "nice." *Pretty*, *cute*, and *nice* don't belong in the studio. But I don't care. I'm nice, I like pretty, and cute never hurt anybody.

"Hey, Trina."

Princess Di wave. "Hey."

26

Ignore

LETICIA

Leticia: Its on.
Bea: OMG!!!
Leticia: At 2:45. Coming?
Bea: <Ignore>
Leticia: R U coming?
Bea: Did U tell Her?
Leticia: <Ignore>
Bea: Did U tell Her?
Leticia: <Ignore>
Bea: TSha tell Her.
Leticia: <Ignore>
Bea: TSHA!!!

27

Bing, Bang, Boom

DOMINIQUE

BING, BANG, BOOM. BING, BANG, BOOM. Six triangles on my essay. Black ink dug deep in the margin. Bing, bang, boom. A chain of black triangles. Didn't know I was doing it. Making them. Linking them. Can't stop myself. Why stop now? Might as well go to the end. Down to the last line. Seven. Eight. Bing, bang, boom.

It doesn't matter which book we read. *The Red Badge of Courage* or *Of Mice and Men*. She asks the same questions. We write the same essay. At least I do. It's all the same triangle:

Point of No Return

Rising Action   Falling Action

Bang

Bing   Boom

I felt bad for Lennie in *Of Mice and Men*. Lennie was set up. He had to do what he did. Even if it was an accident, it had to go down like that. It was all set in motion from jump. I put that down in my essay. Wrote it out, piece by piece. The rising action. How George set Lennie up. How he was supposed to have Lennie's back but he didn't. That was all Steinbeck. Steinbeck set Lennie up. Made him big, dumb, and too strong for his own good. Made him like soft things. Made him kill every soft thing he touched. What choice did Lennie have? What else was he going to do when that soft blonde flit came shaking her blonde curls in his face? Putting her blonde curls in his hands for him to grab. Big, strong, and dumb. Kill every mouse, every puppy, every soft thing. Steinbeck did that. Made Lennie too strong, too dumb, and Lennie couldn't stop himself. It had to play out that way. Point of no return. He didn't have no one looking out for him. Not really. Not George. Not Steinbeck. No one. Then who comes and tells him to close his eyes? Tells him to dream about the rabbits. Soft rabbits. And Lennie's crying, man. Big, dumb, strong, and crying like a weak little bitch. And who takes him out? Who pumps a Luger full of lead into Lennie? Who? The one who's supposed to be his boy. And I wrote that down in the essay. All of it. I laid it out under falling action. *Bing, bang, boom.*

28

Truth in Art

TRINA

"ARTISTS, WHEN YOU HAVE A SHOWING, let the work speak for itself. The patrons will study, admire, question, like, or strongly dislike. Let them. It's art."

I stand out in the gallery, shining like one hot, bright star, loving my artwork. Mr. Sebastian forgot to say love. How can you not love what I'm giving? Harriet Tubman has never worn a more colorful dress. "I Have a Dream" never looked so dreamy. How's this for the language of art?: All of my art has a point of view, and look! Just look. Pretty, pretty, *mmmwack!* Pretty. Sorry, Mr. Sebastian: Pretty, *bonita*, and *linda* are the right words!

"That doesn't look like Malcolm."

I gasp. "Bite your tongue, it does."

Ivan and I go back and forth—does, does not. His art

is good if you like cartoons, Japanese kids with big eyes, and comic book heroes.

Ivan is little-brother cute so I have to tease him. He blushes too easily. I sing, "Someone's eyes are gree-een. Someone's eyes are gree-een." He says I'm tripping but I'm no stranger to the jealous, green-eyed monster. What?

I say, "You wish you could create like this."

He accuses me of sniffing paint fumes. Funny. Too funny. But he's staring at my belly and he isn't looking for my appendix scar. What did I tell you?

I wouldn't want to peek inside his sketch pad. I don't want to see his drawings of me. Even worse, drawings of us. I can imagine what he has us doing. But I'm used to little boys. I know he's deep down suffering for me. I can't do nothing about that. Face it. If I treat him to the famous Trina shaky-shake, we will have a disgusting puddle of boy right at the gallery underneath my magnificent showing. Instead I respect him as an artist and share my process.

I tell him how I took a big picture of Malcolm from the library. Then I hit ENLARGE on the photocopier. Then I took it home, and with my special mix—sorry, secret—I painted over the face. Then, when it dried, I took the face and cut it up. You know. Cubes. Rectangles. Picasso. Then I painted the different parts of the face in black and red because Malcolm was assassinated, you know, so blood is red, his hair was red, so red was my theme. Anyone who rents the movie X will see my point of view right away.

Ivan says, "That's wack."

Oh my God! My face is turning colors. I'm hot and sweating and it reminds me of my appendix bursting.

I don't let myself get hot and angry like this. I don't let people do that to me. Instead I do what I do when people hate on me. I turn them off, *click*, drown out their negativity, and tell myself loud, loud, loud I have talent and aptitude. Yes. Aptitude. *Habilidad*.

I caress his face from the cheek to the chin. So smooth. He has a way to go before becoming a man. I say, "So young. So immature."

He wipes away the trace of my finger. Even though we're the same age, I know through Ivan what it's like to have a little brother. But it works. He is madder than I was a second ago so I win.

Ivan, a boy who draws his head on musclemen's bodies, can't stand it. What? He wants to get back at me. Green eyes don't lie. He wants to start up about Rosa and Harriet, but that's too much in one day and Mr. Sebastian is ready to begin. I leave Ivan in the gallery.

I try to close the door behind me but Ivan doesn't stay left for long. He follows me into the studio over to our worktable. There is enough room for him to work elsewhere, but who does he want to sit with? What a puppy dog.

There's only two charcoal pencils on each worktable. They're already sharpened. Mr. Sebastian doesn't believe in wasting time standing at the sharpener so he prepares everything before each class. Even our sketch pads are waiting for us.

Every year Mr. Sebastian sells one of his paintings and uses the money for our art supplies. He gets us the best stuff. Professional. What? Feel the sketch paper. The bumps. Excuse me, excuse me. Texture. Once you caress the paper you don't want to draw stupidness, tear out and crumple up the sheets. It isn't throwaway paper. And there is the newspaper article on the wall about Mr. Sebastian selling his painting. You care about the paper. I do.

I try to make him smile. I give him the goodness that is Trina but he won't let me break through. He isn't easy like Shel-E-Shel. When I break through Mr. Sebastian we will both be glad. Here he is, Mr. Art Man with a studio down under the Brooklyn Bridge, all of this art, all of these colors, paints, pens, pencils, and music, and you would think happy. Young. Right? I have never seen serious like Mr. Sebastian. Personally I think Mr. Sebastian has a broken heart. His fiancée told him the baby isn't his. His best friend is dying a horrible death. Mr. Sebastian is too serious. Too sad.

"Artists!" he says. "Sit facing your tablemate."

Ivan and I face each other. His eyes are still green with envy. My eyes sparkle at him.

"It's portrait day. For this period one of you will pose and one will draw. Next period, switch."

I raise my hand. Before he calls on me I blurt out, "Where are the colored pencils, Mr. Sebastian?"

He shakes his head. "In your charcoal."

"You mean he"—I point to my annoying *hermanito*— "will draw me black and white and I'll draw him black and white? That's all? That's all?"

Now, you will not believe this. There is a smile on Mr. Sebastian's face. He should do it more often, but that's not the point. I give him crazy point of view, surrealism, cubes, unheard-of mixes for the color brown, and for those I get a nod and a "Good." But I want color and for this he cracks a smile.

In a cartoon voice, Ivan laughs, "An-hanh."

I hear what Mr. Sebastian says about shading and dark and light. I have all of that in my notes. I comprehend. I get it. I just need a color. One color. Green for Ivan's eyes. Isn't art about the truth? Ivan is so jealous of my space in the gallery and it's killing him. He's green. I'm good, but I can't squeeze emerald out of charcoal.

This isn't the end of my problems. Only the beginning. How is he supposed to draw me without hot pink and crème and my lucky gold chain? My hair, my light brown eyes. The natural rose in my lips. Disaster! Disaster! I hate to say it, but there won't be any truth in art. For seventh period we'll all be liars.

Ivan cheeses at me. "What you want to do, Boo? Pose or draw?"

He's getting me back.

Right now I'm thanking Mami for making me *la única*. Maybe my brother or sister wouldn't have the same father as I and maybe they wouldn't be as gorgeous. I can't see fighting all day long with a sibling. I can't deal with all that jealousy.

It's too bad this is a class, a studio of serious artists. It's too bad none of my guys are here to look out for me. Jonesy, Malik, and them. Devin, Eduardo. Ramón, Justin. All my guys. If I gave the word, made the pout, they would take care of me. Talk to Ivan, and Ivan would chill out and mature.

I collect myself. No need to lose control. Everything's good. I'm good.

"I'll be the artist." I pick up the charcoal pencil. I can make a charcoal sketch pretty. I'll enjoy making Ivan pretty.

He turns to his left, his right. He does thug-life, Hollywood, and then Rodin poses. "Go 'head, Boo. Sketch."

29

A Worthless Treaty

LETICIA

UP UNTIL NOW, James Brown, the Godfather of Soul, has stayed out of my head. He lets me eat my lunch, go to the girls' room, and take a class or two without telling me what I need to do. The Godfather of Soul and I are cool until I see Jessie and Turtle in the hallway, working on new steps for tomorrow's fifteen seconds of "Get Up, Get into It, Get Involved." There are so many bodies crowded around them that I can't get through and am forced to watch them dance. Jessie points to Turtle and Turtle points to Jessie, each one telling the other, "You get involved, You get involved. . . ."

Now I'm stuck.

Why couldn't James Brown be content to stay pushed back where I stash lost homework and diet tips?

You, get involved

You, get involved

You, get involved

I fight to push past the crowd gathered around the dancing duo. Half of the crowd provides the chanting on behalf of James Brown. Try getting that out of your head. Try getting through these halls without elbows, backpacks, attitude, a lot of running, and now dancing. There are thirty-five hundred students in this school. The guidance counselors spread the schedules out as best as they can, but there are still thirty-five hundred of us. Some are like Bea—go to school one week, work the next week. Some come in period one (or zero), out period eight, others come in period two, out nine, in period three and out period ten. From period three to period eight you have the weight of the world marching in this cereal box. Can you feel the rumble? That's seven-thousand-odd feet stomping during the bell change. And that's just the stomping. Don't forget about the running, pushing, play fighting, and dancing. School's a dangerous place if you don't know how to get where you're supposed to be.

Mr. Yerkewicz is the only teacher I beat to the classroom. He just drags along, his eyes glassy, his mouth slack and drooly. Drags along in the mix. It is a wonder no one has knocked him down. He just keeps dragging until he makes it to his classroom.

Honestly, if I had a heart attack or stroke I wouldn't be back here. I wouldn't try to fight the stream. I would sue the school and watch TV at home. The school is wrong. They shouldn't make Yerkewicz switch rooms during bell change. I don't know how that man stays on his feet but he does.

Last year, when I was a freshman, Miss Olenbach caught me in the hall during homeroom and asked me to do her a favor. Go collect Delaney cards from rooms 321 through 330. I said okay and went up to the third floor and collected the Delaney cards from 321 and 322. But when I opened the door to room 323 I was barely inside when Mr. Yerkewicz's face turned tomato red and he went down. He just slumped to the floor. He wasn't breathing right and his eyes were wide-open. I was in shock. The whole class was in shock. Everyone stood around saying "Oh shit," and stuff like that. I calmed down, whipped out Celina, hit 3 on speed dial, and started telling Bea what was happening. She started hollering in my ear while I tried to calm her down, but she wouldn't calm down. She kept saying "Do something, Leticia. Do something."

Bea must have been loud because someone in the class heard her voice and ran for help. The principal, the nurse, the school police, and a teacher's aide all rushed to the scene. It was like watching a reality-TV crisis show. I've never seen so many people move so fast in real life. The nurse was on top of Mr. Yerkewicz giving mouth-to-mouth. She wasn't worried about his saliva, his cigar smoking, or his stiff body. She flung herself into the role of nurse, punching his chest and blowing into his mouth as if cameras were rolling. It was thrilling. Sirens were blasting outside, the EMS workers arrived, and the crew came inside and shoved the school nurse off of Yerkewicz. They slapped an oxygen mask over Yerkewicz's face, strapped him onto a gurney, and went racing down the hall knocking onlookers out of the way.

It was happening faster than I could tell Bea, who kept saying "Don't let him die, God. Please, don't let him die."

"Calm down, Bea," I said. "You don't even know that man."

Bea gets involved like she's reading the true-to-life dramas in one of her novels. She can't help it. That's Bea.

At that moment I couldn't worry about Mr. Yerkewicz because I had my own drama to deal with. In the middle of my calming Bea down, Principal Bates tore Celina, my little girl, from my hands. One minute Celina was cradled to my ear, the next minute my warm little

Celina was ripped away. I almost had a heart attack on the spot. I was no good for the rest of the day.

Finally at 3:00—yep, had me waiting fifteen minutes—Principal Bates returned my little girl to me and told me not to bring her back to school. I said, "I promise," and took my baby back, wiped her down good, and charged her up when I got home.

Mr. Yerkewicz drops his books on the teacher's desk, picks up the chalk, and writes Treaty of Versailles on the board. I'm so through with French following me from class to class that I say nice and loud, "Ver-frickin-si," while Yerkewicz writes. I could have said much worse, for all Yerkewicz cares. He would keep on dragging his feet across the floor and the chalk across the board.

His handwriting isn't so good. You can only make out the first and last letter of each word. Everything else is just curves, dots, and squiggles. Neither his feet nor the chalk lift, but that doesn't stop him from doing his job. He writes those notes on the board as if we could read them. The objective, the outline, and tonight's reading. Then he starts talking about Versailles, and at any given moment he says, "Versailles. The worthless treaty," like Worthless Treaty is its middle name. There's a low rumble of laughter, but honestly, I doubt he hears us laughing or cares. He doesn't even ask questions, check if we've done the reading, or take attendance. Lorna fills out his Delaney card and walks it down to the office. Yerkewicz just writes and talks. He stands in front of us like he's standing on the Verrazano Bridge looking out at our faces like we're the green-blue ocean. And while he's talking he shakes his head, chuckles, and says like it's a tragedy, "Versailles, the worthless treaty." Then, before the bell goes off, he says, "Those French didn't stand a chance."

30

Duncan, Bench

DOMINIQUE

WE SHOULD HAVE WON LAST NIGHT'S GAME. That game was rocking. We were down nine points. If I could have just got in there. . . . Clock was ticking down and I looked to Coach,

looked to Coach,

looked to Coach,

praying she would change her mind. Put me in. They scored a 3 with no one checking for the J. I jumped up off the bench and Coach said, "Duncan, down."

I could read the other team. Read the zone. I could have jumped in there and checked their point guard. Number Six was fast. Had a sweet no-look pass, but I was onto her; I could read her.

Aw, man. Coach was killing me. Killing me. I had to jump in there. Shut Six down. But Coach had me benched.

"Why you doing this to me?"

Coach didn't look my way once. "Bench" is what she told me. "Duncan, bench."

I was getting more heated by the minute. Heated by the basket. And they were scoring on us. Spanking us in our own court. Down nine, eleven, thirteen. The game was slipping through Ellen's non-ball-handling fingers. All Coach would say was "Stay down, Duncan. Duncan, bench."

"Coach, let me in. Let me turn it around." There was still time. With eight minutes left, I could've jumped in there. Made things happen. Not even Reese and Bishop could have won this for us. Ellen couldn't put the ball in their hands. Aw, man. The ball in my hands would've been the ball in their hands.

Coach wouldn't hear me or see me. I was dismissed. Invisible. Coach only saw her clipboard, her plays, her non-ball-handling Ellen. Yeah. The all-arounder. The scholar-service-athlete. Miss Who's Who Shoot and Miss.

Game to game, I gave Coach triple-doubles, but "Bench, Duncan" was what I got. That's right. Ride that bench, Duncan. Stay. Sit. Know your place.

Damn. I'm not invisible. Why couldn't Coach see me? My dribble is tight. *Slam/slam/slam*. Like a drumroll spanking that hardwood. I wanted in. Needed in. Had to jump in there and go man to man against Number Six. If she stuck her hand between the slam I'da had something for her.

I couldn't watch Ellen dribbling scared. I swear, she didn't own a pair. I was sick. Ill. Mad. Watching her dribbling scared. No ball-handling skills. No tight slam/slam/slam. She couldn't even see free hands behind her or free hands to the side. But there she was, dribbling loose down the lane waiting to be mugged, and Six was all over it for the easy pick.

"Please, Coach," I said. "Let me in. Sit her down and let me in."

Coach's hand went up, a big-ass stop sign: "Duncan. Bench."

That was all I got. For all my assists. All my steals. For making fouls when we needed to, for sinking foul shots, I was invisible to her. Invisible. Duncan. Bench. Duncan. Bench. And all I wanted was the ball. The ball, the court. The ball, the court.

Coach doesn't have to look up. She knows it's me standing in the door frame. She waves me in.

"Why you doing this, Coach?" I ask. "Why you benching me?"

"You know my rules," Coach says. "Seventy-five to take the floor."

"But I need to play. I need my minutes."

"Look, Duncan. I'm not in control of that. You are. Kick up your grades and I'll play you."

"I can't wait for that. Season will be over by then."

She shrugs. "You'll play next season."

This is all so simple to her. No big thing to her. But it's life to me and she's not hearing me. Not seeing me.

Coach is wrong. It's not how she says it is. I don't control shit. I don't control Hershheiser. The grades I get. The classes on my schedule. When I come and go. I don't control none of that. All of that's controlling me. Boxing me in.

The only thing I control is the ball. Steal it. Dribble. Pass it. Shoot it. I control the ball. Control the court. That's what I control.

"Just let us fight for it. Ellen and me. See who starts and who sits."

Now my heart is sloppy hanging out. My knees are scraping the rug from all this crawling. This isn't nothing but simple to her. A simple rule that she controls. And I'm begging like a dumb bitch getting kicked to the curb. And I'm trying to get her to see, to hear me out, and she says, "We're done, Duncan. Get to class."

31

Girl Most Secretly

TRINA

THEY SHOULD HAVE A NEW CATEGORY in the yearbook when I graduate: Girl Most Secretly Sketched. Ivan doesn't know how blessed he is. Every person holding a charcoal pencil in this studio steals glances at our worktable. My neck is stiff but these eyes don't miss a thing. Shamel, Lizette, Pradeep, and them want to change models. They must wonder, Why can't we draw Trina? and who can blame them.

I give him so much to work with from any angle he chooses to study me. Even if he has no imagination whatsoever, all he has to do is follow the curve of my cheekbones and lips, get the sparkle in my light brown eyes, the point of my cute nose, and he can't go wrong. And this hair? What? I let it fall to my shoulders so he can pick up the natural shine. I am too nice. Does Ivan know what a gift I'm giving him and his sketch pad?

Our art program is filled with lonely boys. Lonely boys who take to drawing because talking doesn't come easily. They don't create color and art like I do. Instead they take Mr. Sebastian's art paper, the paper he sold his paintings for, and draw cartoons with big eyes, mondo missile tatas, musclemen, and monsters. Little lonely boys.

My butt is numb and I want to get up, shaky-shake and stomp, from the head to the booty to the toe. Like in the caf with the Boosters. But I keep posing, keep giving, and then for no reason Ivan goes crazy. He takes that charcoal pencil and circles round and round on the pad. I freak. He's messing me up.

"What are you doing?"

Do you know what Ivan has the nerve to say? Do you?

"Mr. Sebastian," he calls out, "the model's talking. She's breaking the aura."

I know I am supposed to be art, but art for incredible inspiration. Not a bowl of fruit. A dumb cat.

Mr. Sebastian doesn't even come over to handle the situation. He just bellows from Pradeep's table, "Trina . . ."

Ivan keeps making round, round circles with that

black charcoal pencil. What can he do that's round, round, round on my face and needs so much black?

"Oval," I say from my gut through my teeth, because I'm trying to stay still. Trying to be professional. "Oval, not *round*."

I don't have to turn to see people shifting to look this way. And there's giggling. I don't appreciate being looked at and laughed at.

But what does Mr. Sebastian say? You guessed it. As if it's my fault, all my fault. "Trina . . ."

Am I burning?

Here is my wonderful, wonderful day, my hot-pink near-perfection day, and Ivan has to put a smudge on my day. On my star.

I thought Ivan had a crush on me but he turns out to be another hater. Hah. And I drew his portrait to perfection and with a little fun. Just wait. I'm going to give him a complete makeover and rip his face out of my expensive artist's sketch pad.

That black charcoal in his hand goes round, round, round. My face isn't round. Isn't charcoal black. I am screaming inside. Screaming. And clawing Ivan's eyes out of their sockets.

"You're trembling, Boo. Be still. I got you. I got you."

Oh my God. Did you see? Did you? His lips blowing

a kiss at me? Hah. Who does he think he is?

Green, green, green. Hater, hater, hater.

Get here quick, Sebastian. Come and see what he's doing.

If Ivan gets the nod, like "Good," like Sebastian gives me, I'll relax. If he gives Ivan the "That's enough" stare-down, then I'll freak because the face on the pad is a joke.

No. Even better. Let Ivan make his comic book joke of me. I'll tell Mr. Sebastian *he* has to draw me. And then sell it for hundreds—no, thousands—to pay for art supplies next year. It could go in the school brochure to talk about the art program.

Yes, yes, yes! Draw me, Mr. Sebastian. Draw me.

Finally Sebastian stops messing around with everyone else and he's at our table. He opens my sketch pad, finds my portrait of Ivan, nods. Okay. I'm used to it. Typical. I have something smart for Ivan but I keep it in my mouth.

Mr. Sebastian stands behind Ivan. His eyes go to me first and then down to the sketch pad. No nod or "Good" like I get. Instead Ivan gets "Hmm." And the eyebrows go up. Mr. Sebastian actually moved the upper part of his face for Ivan's drawing. Ivan got face movement. And a "Hmm."

I don't know what to think. I know the portrait is beautiful. What else can it be? But my face isn't round like that or black like that. I have color. Perfect blended color. And my shape is oval, and maybe a little heart shaped. But not round. Just because the portrait is beautiful doesn't make it right, and I am disappointed in Mr. Sebastian. This is the art place. Art is beauty and beauty is truth and my face isn't round.

And why do I get "Good" and a nod, and Ivan gets "Hmm" and the eyebrows?

My day, my wonderful, hot-pink, set-to-star day was almost perfect. Now it has a smudge on it. A round charcoal smudge.

32

Band Practice at Three

LETICIA

I CAN FEEL CELINA PURRING THROUGH MY BAG. It's a text purr, not a calling purr. I don't open my bag to look inside. I know who it is. I know who keeps texting, pestering, and stressing me.

Did U tell her?	
Do something.	YOU get involved
Theres time.	YOU get involved
Tell her TSha.	YOU get involved
Clean your mess.	YOU get involved

I'm all jittery and can't settle myself. I hear Chem II James talking but it might as well be Bridgette running the vacuum cleaner in the other room: I know there's sound, but it's all in the background.

I'm supposed to be helping James along, getting this party started, making the most of these two minutes before Mr. Cosgrove takes control of the class and before the unbalanced equations get so complicated. I have to be present, all ears and mind, but I'm too cluttered to be present. Too cluttered for James or for Chem II. There's too many voices screaming at me all at once and I can't, I just can't—

"I said, 'Leticia, why you stressing?' "

He's smiling at me and I can't even roll around in the bliss of it. I just wish he would sit down and leave me alone. Just let me work out these jitters and calm myself down.

"I got it," he says. It's a face full of charm. One day I'll replay it all and be la-la-ed out, but right now I'm thinking we're incompatible. He's not catching my vibe. This will never work.

James doesn't know he's being cut loose. Still smiling, he says, "You have band practice at three."

"Band practice?"

"Band practice." He points to the pen in my hand—my damaged hand—and says, "You've been hitting the desk to the beat. Either you're drumming with the sophomore band or something's on your mind."

Gasp! I close my hand quick and stash it under my

desk, not believing I had my damaged hand exposed for everyone to see.

"There's nothing on my mind."

He won't leave me alone. He puts his big hands on my shoulders, presses down hard, and squeezes. "Girl, you're tight."

On any other day I would have let him massage my shoulders until Mr. Cosgrove made him stop. I'm not the kind of girl who turns down pampering. But right now I don't want to be bothered and I wrestle my shoulders out of his grip.

He gets the message. Chem II James sits down.

CALL ME	Everybody right there!
CALL ME	Everybody right there!
TELL HER	Get involved. Get involved.

That does it! I am through! When the bell rings at 2:45, Celina, I am putting you to bed permanently. All this crying every two minutes. I can't turn off everything in my ear but I can turn you off.

James turns to look at me. Milton turns to look at me. Nettie, then Justin, then Brian, and now the whole class is staring at me. Then Mr. Cosgrove starts walking

down the aisle, not dancing to a ringtone, just walking.
He bends down and takes my hand. My damaged hand.

"What's going on, Leticia?"

I look down. I can't stop the pen from tapping.

33

Jumped

LETICIA

THE BELL RINGS and I just want to bust out Chem II and out of school, period. Just let me get to the Golden Blossom Nail Salon and take care of my emergency. Once I'm planted in that cushy gold chair, with my fingers soaking in the soapy liquid, and Girl Number Four with the mole on her left earlobe is rubbing my damaged hand, I can relax, say, "Ahhh," because everything will be all right.

I'm fighting to get down B Corridor but there's a thousand feet marching and a thousand kids pushing. And there goes Trina, bouncing and smiling her big-cheese grin. The crowd is with her, carrying everyone along in the stream of excited, pushing kids. And I know she thinks this is a parade and she's the beauty queen in the center of her own float. And the door pushes open and she walks outside and—

TRINA

Sun is still out on this cold, cold day but they're chanting my name, "Trina, Trina," and it's—

DOMINIQUE

There she is. I got her. I got her.

LETICIA

Oh my God!

I see gold spinning and pink flying. Trina getting slammed down on that concrete. The crowd is swarming like one body around all this mess and—

TRINA

"Hhhuaaawhhhaaat?"

Jonesy! Malik! Mikki! Eduardo! Nilda! I see them all around. Everyone. They're there. All around. I'm reaching out to them. Reaching . . .

LETICIA

Celina screams and I don't even say, "Who?" I flip Celina open and say, "Dominique's wilding out on Trina. She's punching the shit out of her. Trina's down and Dominique's punching her—ooooh—face!

"OhmyGod, that girl is bleeding and Dominique won't let up. She's messing her up, saying—"

DOMINIQUE

"You see me, bitch?

"You see me, bitch?

"You see my face now, bitch?"

LETICIA

"What? What?

"The crowd is crazy. I can't hear a word you're—"

DOMINIQUE

Get offa me.
  Get offa me.
  Get offa me, Dyke.

TRINA

Hwhauhmm . . .

LETICIA

"The cops! The cops are here. Yeah. The big lady cop
got Dominique down. Down like they do on TV. Got
her knee in Dominique's back. Got Dominique kissing
concrete. Yeah. They're cuffing her now. Oh my God!
  "Trina? I can't see.
  "Oh, Bea! Oh my God! She's not moving.
  "They took Trina away. The ambulance. Unh-hunh.
Yeah, they got Dominique. Yeah. Squad car."

The minute AP Shelton asks, "Did you see anything?"
people start fleeing every which way. He's headed toward

me, looking dead at me. I don't know what it is about AP Shelton, but our eyes lock.

"Miss Moore," he says, "you seem to know what goes on. What can you tell me?"

"Look, AP Shelton. I'm just trying to get to the nail salon. That's all I'm trying to do."

"So you don't know what happened here?"

"Not really—look. School's out. I gotta go. Nail appointment."

I just keep walking. Talking to Bea.

34

Artist to Artist

IVAN

"YOUR MOMS JUST STEPPED OUT. She's in the chapel. She'll be back."

"I've been sitting here for the longest. I just don't know what to say to you."

"Damn, girl . . . you must be jacked under all those bandages. Messed up. Look at all this hookup. Tubes. Machines beeping. Oxygen tank. You don't know how sci-fi you look. Like an astronaut. A mummified astronaut."

"Hey. You didn't get my face right. That's a lousy thing to say with you lying here like this.

"Yeah. I snuck a peek at your sketch pad. You got some ideas. A few. But you can't do portraits, though. You don't have mines right. You know, artist to artist. You didn't shade my eyes right. Look at these. Dark, Trina. My eyes are dark. You shaded them too light. And the nose. See this thing? Been in my family for generations, but how would you know that? Anyway, you made it too perfect. Like, cute. Gives me hives, girl. Hives. But I liked what you did with the ears. That was mad funny. I got the joke. The little pointy ears. Not too pointy but enough for me to get it. Nice dig. That was funny, man.

"I'm gonna keep on talking, okay? That's what they say. Play music and talk. Familiar sounds. Well, I don't know what you like to hear so I guess I'll just talk until your moms get here."

"Where's your mother, girl? She must be a praying woman. She been in that chapel for an hour and a half. Okay. That's all right. What else is she going to do but pray?"

"You know your stuff's still up. Black History Month's long gone but your crazy Malcolm and Martin, and all those roses, and the old lady in the green dress still hanging in the gallery. Yeah. Your own showing in C Corridor. Extended run. Solo act. Starring Trina."

"Oh. Okay, nurse. Just a sec.

"They booting me out, Boo. Guess they gotta do stuff to you. Check this out. I brought you something. I'm setting it right here. A giant card. Everyone signed it. All your friends. Some teachers. The cops.

"Okay, nurse. A second, a second.

"And I brought your portrait. The one I did. Redid. I'm pinning it on your bulletin board, for when you open your eyes. Thought you'd want to see yourself.

"Yeah, nurse. I know. I'm going. Oh. Check it out. This is what she really looks like."

35
Celebrity

LETICIA

"BEA! BEA! TURN ON THE TV!

"No. Put that book down! Yeah. Channel nine."

Bea can't believe it. Neither can I. Channel Nine News is doing a whole news story about girl-on-girl violence and how it's on the rise for God knows what reason. Pressure is the best they can come up with.

Anyway, it's six months since that drama between Dominique and Trina, and who is on TV, in my bedroom, wearing an orange jumpsuit, talking about how she was "correcting the situation"?

"Check her out!" I holler into Celina. "She is unreal! She's not even sorry!"

Bea is shushing me but this is hot and I'm excited. Here is Dominique, saying "No, I'm not sorry" and "No, I didn't learn anything," being all hard rock.

"Do you hear her?"

"Hush!"

Then the scene switches from the correctional facility to a living room. The newsperson is setting the stage, the way they do, telling the story about a once-promising art student forced to transfer after a violent attack on school grounds. The newsperson talks about the senselessness of it all, the coma, how the victim regained consciousness, the victim's first words, and all the reconstructive surgeries she'll need.

"Oh my God! It's Trina!" Trina, live on TV.

Even though the two people are sitting behind a screen so you can see only their silhouettes, you know it's Trina and her mother. The girl's not hyper and bouncy, but it's Trina. While she's trying to talk, her mother is crying and speaking Spanish. I mean, my Spanish is pretty good but I can't make out a single word. Doesn't matter. The translator is on top of it. Besides, it's not the mother who's hard to understand.

Trina's silhouette says she doesn't know why she was attacked. She remembers seeing everyone around her. All her friends and . . . She can't even talk about getting jumped. She says everything went black.

"Bea. Listen to her. She's not stuttering. It's like her speech is, I don't know—"

"Delayed," Bea says all fast and handy. Then she shushes me again.

It's pathetic. The newsperson wants Trina to talk faster but it's like she can't. Every time she utters a sound it's as if she's learning how to talk. Like she's searching for lost words. She's definitely not all fast and crazy, like old Trina. But you can still hear that it's Trina.

They show her artwork and they talk about how beautiful and confident she once was. Then they show a black-and-white portrait that one of her classmates did. Trina is all over the news. There's even a foundation set up for her. They're flashing the Web site and the toll-free number. She's like a celebrity.

Once the news story goes off, I'm ready to tear into it—I'm good for a few hours' worth of talking—but Bea's going out tonight. Someone new. Yeah. She dumped Jay. And she has to finish her book before her date comes. That's Bea for you. Bea and her true-to-life novels. It's like I lose her every time she picks up a book. So we hang up and I plug Celina back into the charger. We'll talk later.

I keep clicking with the remote, looking for something good. Something juicy. You know, it's by pure luck that I caught Dominique and Trina on channel nine. And I'm like, wow. I finally know real people on television. And to think, I was there when it all went down. I could have been on that news program being interviewed. I knew all about it from start to finish. I just look at the TV and I can't believe it. I just can't believe it.

ACKNOWLEDGMENTS

This novel could not have been written without those who offered support, let me roam their hallways, and gave me a seat in the back of the class: Behind the Book, Beach Channel High School, Benjamin N. Cardozo High School, Brooklyn Community Arts and Media High School, DeWitt Clinton High School, Franklin K. Lane High School, and Thurgood Marshall High School.

To Rosemary Brosnan, who once again gave me space to write.

Turn the page for a behind-the-scenes
look at writing *Jumped*.

JUMPED

Behind the Book:
Rita Williams-Garcia on Writing *Jumped*

A Deleted Scene from the Novel

Beyond the Book:
Activities for Further Discussion

Behind the Book:
Rita Williams-Garcia on Writing *Jumped*

I wrote *Jumped* to examine the role that we all play in peer violence. If we're crowding around fights, we're playing a role. If we're recording, posting, viewing, giving a "playback" of these acts of violence, we're playing a role. No one is exempt.

To date, *Jumped* was my hardest novel. I saw it as a Greek tragedy or tragic comedy with tragically flawed goddesses and unspoken commentary. At first I couldn't get my goddesses to cooperate. I'd hit the keys and they'd punch back at me. Over two years and many rewrites, I began to find them. Understand them. Scold them. Laugh at them. Eventually we came to terms. We made peace.

A Deleted Scene from the Novel

Shopping: Part One
Leticia

The bell rings and we're all pushing our way out into the hallway to get to the next class. A motorized wheelchair comes straight at me and I shout, "Hey! You know you see me."

"Oops," the Wheelchair Guy says. "Sorry."

"No," I tell him as he rolls by, laughing. "You will be sorry." I know his game, all right. Ram into a girl for some jollies and plead blind, because if you don't see, you're not responsible. Well, it's his legs that are handicapped. Not his eyes.

There's a time to not see because everyone else is not seeing, and a time you can't fake it. Stuff is staring you dead in the face so you gotta make a move. Like last summer when Bridget and I were in the city shopping for school clothes.

I had my Shopping: Part One list of must-have pieces. A denim skirt. Six jeans, different colors. Six summer-to-fall tops. One tight cardigan. One light jacket. Three pairs of sneakers: one to walk in, a pair for gym, and a scuffable pair. Since Bridge only had a grand to charge on her American Express, we'd save panties, bras, boots, and a heavy fall jacket for Shopping: Part Two.

So, I was like, "Mommy, let's take the truck because I'm not struggling up and down subway steps with a million packages." Bridget was like, "Heifer, please. Do you know what parking costs in the city? Just deal. We ride the subway train or we don't go." In hindsight, what sense did that make? We planned to spend a grand easy, hooking up the semester. What's an extra thirty dollars on a parking space?

The truth was, Mommy don't like no one touching her precious truck. She would die if a cab scratches or dings her brand-new, hard-earned truck. Bridget made Bernie throw all his stuff out of the garage so nothing could accidentally rub up against her truck. She supervises the guys wiping her windshield at the gas station and the guys washing and waxing her precious monster at the car wash. How anyone can be attached to a thing is beyond me.

Still, since Bridget holds the Amex card, we take the subway to Herald Square. Now, if there's a million cars, buses, and taxis clogging up 34th Street, what do you suppose the sidewalks look like? And here we are, struggling with our bags, right? Trying to get from store to store, from 6th Avenue to 7th Avenue. So we both fall in line and do what everyone else does; I shield my eyes like a bat or a horse with blinders and go on instinct and rhythm. That blinders thing is in full effect, with thousands of people banking off invisible paths, and no one hits no one else. Or at least, not hard. Well, this girl must not have gotten the text, because, BANG, she hits me, a full-on collision. Now, she doesn't acknowledge her fault. Instead, she says, "'Scuse you. Why don't you look?" She was feeling mightier than her ninety-five pounds, standing next to her man. But so what? I had at least a hundred pounds on her, plus Bridget, and I replied, "No, heifer. You look."

And that was the least of it. She was wearing this end-of-summer-outfit that I didn't get a chance to buy yet. I was conflicted between wanting to know where she got those rags and standing up for myself. Then, she says, "You open your eyes. Can't no one walk around your big ass."

People were bumping into us because we were stopping the flow of sidewalk traffic, but I couldn't feel any of that. Scrawny Girl's nerve sent me into a mental tailspin.

Bridget hates trouble and wants to keep moving. Scrawny's boyfriend also seems to hate trouble and tells her to relax. It was too late for all of that. I shoved my bags in Bridget's hands and pushed the girl. Then, Scrawny Girl—in my summer outfit, no less—jumps on me like some alley cat and goes for my hair. Yes. My straight-from-the-salon tresses. I'm just trying to unhook her hands from my hair while she's kicking me. Then Bridget steps in and the boyfriend tries to pull her off, and the crowd swells up around us, and the police show up.

The boyfriend, on parole for sure, was like, "Officers, Officers, it was nothing."

Bridget gives the boyfriend a payback kick, and is like, "Let's just get our stuff and go."

The police officers don't want to do any paper-work, so they're like, "Citizen Jane, go this way, and Citizen Joan, go that way."

The onlookers go back to blindly gliding along the sidewalk and Bridget and I go down in the sub-way with our bags and get on the train. I'm fixing my hair, using the reflection of the opposite window. I can't believe how wild my tresses are looking. I can't believe that Scrawny Girl had the nerve to not see me coming.

Beyond the Book:
Activities for Further Discussion

I have to thank readers for sharing the many ways you're using *Jumped* in your classrooms, libraries, and reading clubs. The first activity comes from teacher Kristy Willis of Junior High School 13 in Manhattan.

• Leticia's, Trina's, and Dominique's lives run along a collision course, and yet the girls never interact, with the exception of the fateful attack. Choose two characters from *Jumped* and write a brief interaction between them. The characters can be two of the main characters or a main and secondary character. Decide whether the interaction will bring clarity or tension to the events leading up to or following the attack.

• Put Leticia, Trina, and Dominique on trial for the roles they play in the attack. Have prosecutor(s) ask the defendants questions while each character defends herself. Use secondary characters as witnesses. Include a judge to moderate the proceedings and a jury panel to form an opinion.

• Perform Reader's Theater. First create a short script by taking brief excerpts from different chapters. Feel free to cut out extraneous words or passages in the narrative or dialogue. Organize the excerpts in order to create a dramatic presentation. For example, create a one-woman show by selecting several passages that show a particular character's development. Create a dynamic reading by finding passages that show each character's outlook on one topic (i.e., clothing, boyfriends, personal responsibility, class participation, etc.), and then stage the order of the excerpts to highlight their different perspectives.

• Trina describes her artwork as colorful with a crazy point of view. Replicate one of her Black History mural portraits using the descriptions of her techniques.

- Trina likens herself to both the artist Picasso and to his work. Visit the art section of your local library to view the works of Picasso. Re-envision Trina or yourself as a Picasso abstract.

- Leticia, Trina, and Dominique are characterized by their interests. Choose one of the main characters and create a collage incorporating their interests and objects associated with them. Try the same activity using yourself as the subject.

- Form an anti-violence teen group at your school. Invite students to talk about being on all sides of violent acts: attackers, targets, and bystanders. In the name of teenage victims of violence, stand up and speak up. Break down the wall of silence.

Have fun!

RITA WILLIAMS-GARCIA's Newbery Honor Book, *One Crazy Summer*, was a winner of the Coretta Scott King Author Award, a National Book Award finalist, the recipient of the Scott O'Dell Award for Historical Fiction, and a *New York Times* bestseller. The two sequels, *P.S. Be Eleven* and *Gone Crazy in Alabama*, were both Coretta Scott King Author Award winners and ALA Notable Children's Books. She is also the author of *A Sitting in St. James*, National Book Award finalist *Clayton Byrd Goes Underground*, *Blue Tights*, Coretta Scott King Honor Book *Like Sisters on the Homefront*, and four ALA Best Books for Young Adults: *Jumped*, a National Book Award finalist; *No Laughter Here*; *Every Time a Rainbow Dies*, a *Publishers Weekly* Best Children's Book; and *Fast Talk on a Slow Track*. Rita Williams-Garcia lives in Jamaica, New York. You can visit her online at www.ritawg.com.